BURNT WAGON RANCH

'Milk River'—that was the password, as Darr Gardner and his gunslicks rode into town at dawn. The men were tough and ready, and Gardner had given them their orders: 'Shoot to kill—and kill every farmer you see. This time we're wipin' them out for good!' That was the beginning of a day of slaughter such as the town of Burnt Wagon had never seen— and would never see again.

BURNT WAGON RANCH

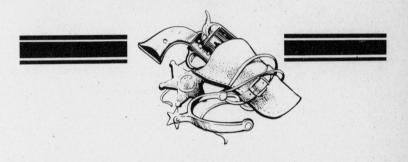

Lee Floren

ATLANTIC LARGE PRINT
Chivers Press, Bath, England.
John Curley & Associates Inc.,
South Yarmouth, Mass., USA.

Library of Congress Cataloging in Publication Data

Floren, Lee.
 Burnt Wagon Ranch.

 (Atlantic large print)
 1. Large type books.   I. Title.
 [PS3511.L697B8   1986]   813'.52   85–17135
 ISBN 0–89340–968–5 (Curley: lg. print)

British Library Cataloguing in Publication Data

Floren, Lee
 Burnt Wagon Ranch.—Large print ed.
 I. Title
 813'.52[F]   PS3511.L697

 ISBN 0–7451–9110–X

This Large Print edition is published by Chivers Press, England, and
John Curley & Associates, Inc, U.S.A. 1986

Published by arrangement with Donald MacCampbell, Inc
U.K. Hardback ISBN 0 7451 9110 X
U.S.A. Softback ISBN 0 89340 968 5

Photoset, printed and bound in Great Britain by
REDWOOD BURN LIMITED, Trowbridge, Wiltshire

TO ROBERT

BURNT WAGON RANCH

CHAPTER ONE

He was twenty-four, a well dressed young man, and he had a bony face—a wide forehead, blue eyes, and a strong nose and jaw. He played a card and said, 'Let's see you take that trick, Jake.'

'I'll take it,' Jake said, and he did.

Buckley Wilson pushed back his cream-colored Stetson and said, 'Holy Smoke, you sure did. Now what kind of a partner have I got?' He looked at the square-faced farmer who sat opposite him.

'I'm not that good,' the farmer said, smiling.

They were playing whist in Buckley Wilson's office, there on Burnt Wagon's main street. They were farmers, all of them, even Buck Wilson. Buck had located the three of them on their farms, for he was a land locator. Besides being a land locator, he also had taken up a homestead, out on Diamond Willow Creek, six miles north of Burnt Wagon.

Outside, the rain swept across the Montana earth, bringing the promise of green grass and growing crops.

Buck listened, and said, 'That rain sure sounds good to this boy's ears, men.'

1

'I've got all my wheat sowed,' Jake said. 'Just got done yesterday when the first drops started to fall.'

Another farmer said, 'You always was lucky, Jake. I still have twenty-odd acres to sow yet. Not wheat, though; barley. I'll need some cowfeed come this winter. Well, try to take that, Buck.'

Buck studied the card, said, 'You win again. Shucks, I still have sixty acres to sow, but you don't hear me bellyaching. I'm danged glad it's raining, even if all my land isn't in crop yet.'

'There'll still be time to raise a crop,' another man said, playing a card. 'Well, what do you say, Jake?'

Jake looked at the card. 'I say nothing, Smitty.'

There was an air of conviviality in the small room that was fogged by cigar and tobacco smoke. Of the four men, only Buck Wilson had been raised in this Burnt Wagon region—his father, Charles Wilson, had once run cattle here, and he'd run a big ranch, too, until the terrible winter of 1881 and 1882 had broken his Bar S outfit.

At that time, there had been only two big cow outfits in this Burnt Wagon section of Montana Territory—one had been Charlie Wilson's Bar S and the other had been Wade

2

McMahan's Rafter Y spread. The winter had driven Buck's dad out of the cattle business, for when the snow had finally fallen before a Chinook wind, Bar S cattle, bloated and stinking, had been ugly dots on the brown Montana earth, victims of the worst winter the plain country had ever witnessed.

Wade McMahan's Rafter Y had pulled through, existed for a few years, then had been forced to sell out to a Texas outfit, which kept the same iron, the Rafter Y. Darr Gardner had bought the Rafter Y for a song, driven in Texas cattle, and had become the only big cow outfit in this range.

Darr Gardner had owned the Rafter Y about a year when the Montana Pacific built its grade and laid rails through Burnt Wagon Basin.

And since then, nobody had known peace.

Jake said, playing a card, 'Heard the hide buyer was in town. Me, I got a few hides to sell him—skinned them off some winter-killed stock of mine. Also got a few muskrat an' beaver pelts I trapped in the crick. My play, eh?'

'Best get shut of them muskrats an' beavers afore the warm weather slips the hair on 'em.' A farmer squinted at his cards. 'I done heard that Darr Gardner and Len Huff is aimin' to run thet hide buyer out, they tells me.'

3

Buck played, said, 'I heard that too.'

For a long minute nothing was said. There were two sounds—the shuffle of cards, the rain on the roof. Each man had his own thoughts, and each found a discordant note running through those thoughts. It repeated and repeated, an old, ugly refrain of hate and greed and lust.

'That hide buyer would have had a field day had the Rafter Y skinned their dead critters,' a farmer said, eyeing his cards. 'Darrell Gardner had a big winter kill, but shucks, he never had a one of his dead cows skinned. Jes' left 'em where they fell, he did.'

'Them hides'd be jest chicken feed for him,' Jake put in.

Buck squinted over his cigarette's smoke at his cards. He seemed to be drawing bad hands today. Maybe it was because his mind wasn't on the game.

The fall before, in conjunction with the Montana Pacific, he had located six farmers on Burnt Wagon range. Two years ago the winter had been rather hard and long. Yet it was mild compared to the winter of the big kill, and he had expected the past one to be mild. It had proved to be harder than the previous winter, much to his disappointment and the sorrow of the new farmers he had moved in on what had been Rafter Y grass.

4

Darr Gardner had said, 'This winter will drive them hoemen outa this country. They'll lose their stock an' be plumb busted come spring.'

He was a hard, big man, this Darr Gardner. About thirty, a man would guess—his life had been hard, and this was reflected on his heavy, tough-looking face. He weighed about two hundred, maybe a few pounds over. Those pounds, though, were bone and muscle—big bones and big muscles.

Rumor held that Darrell Gardner was a *Tejano* renegade. Rumor whispered other things: it told of a trailherd being highjacked on the Dodge City Trail, but no evidence had ever been gathered that would take Darr Gardner into Montana Territorial Court.

Rumor also had a few whispers concerning Len Huff. Huff was a thin, deadly man of about forty-five, maybe older. Quiet, soft-spoken, he had a way of looking at a man like he didn't see him, and all the time that smile of his would be forming, a deadly smile.

Dame Rumor held that Len Huff was also a Texas *renegado*, run out of the Lone Star State. But no man made friends with Len Huff, who rodded Darr Gardner's big Rafter Y outfit, running the wagons out on calf roundup and beef roundup. Maybe Len Huff

5

wasn't as tough as word pictured him. Maybe he was tougher than that.

So far, no man had tested him.

Buckley Wilson leaned back in his homemade chair and squinted at his cards. Same hand he had had the last round, only worse.

'Who dealt these?'

Jake said, 'I did. Why?'

'Your mother ought to be ashamed of you.'

'Maybe she is,' Jake replied. 'She died right young.'

'Havin' you as a son,' said Buck, 'would be a terrible shock to a mother.'

Jake said, 'How about me for a husband?'

'Your wife left you, you told me.'

Jake smiled, his eyes sharp. 'Yep, that she did.' He played a card. 'Married only a week, we was, over in Kaintuck. She done run off with a butcher. Hey, Buck, you won a hand!'

Buck said, 'Who'd've imagined it?'

Jake Jones studied his partner. 'By the way, son, you ain't so nice for a man's eyes.'

'He's got two women after him,' Smitty said.

Buck blushed a little. 'Let's leave women outa this. Let's talk about some neutral thing, like the rain.'

But still his thoughts kept going back to Darr Gardner and Len Huff, and the big

6

Rafter Y.

According to his way of thinking, the time of the big cowman was over with, done with. The Homestead Act had opened the way for farmers to come into the West and settle. The Great Northern railroad had built into Montana, running along the Milk River until it darted west of Pacific Junction, heading for Marias Pass in the Rockies. The Northern Pacific also ran its rails across Montana. And the railroads had received land grants, too.

These had cut into open range. With cattle at a low price, a man could not make much money running cows if he had to pay taxes on his land. Running on government land, up to now the cowmen had been free of all taxation. Now, that was ending, for with the railroads stretching steel ribs across the Territory, farmers could ship their produce east to the big cities.

And farmers were squeezing out the big cow outfits.

Cowmen and cowboys derisively called them 'Sodbusters' and 'pun'kin rollers' and 'hoemen' and 'plow pushers.' They held derision toward the farmers—the age-old derision that a horseman has always held for the plodder on foot. But some of the cowboys, thinking along the lines of Buckley Wilson, had sold their saddles for plows, and were

7

farming.

The Big Kill had completely broken Buck and his dad. And old Charlie Wilson had spent his lifetime building up his Bar S. The shock of the complete wipe-out in the winter of 1881–82 had helped hurry old Charlie to his grave.

Buck had gone over to the Black Hills, about six hundred miles away, and punched cows there for a while, even doing a little prospecting, but his thoughts had always been centered, so it seemed, around the place of his birth—Burnt Wagon Basin. So he had come back and filed on a homestead.

Darr Gardner had asked, 'You gone loco, Buckley?'

'Not quite,' Buck had returned.

Gardner had sat his big sorrel gelding, the bronc pulling at the bit. And beside the gelding had been the bay of Len Huff. Huff had not said a word. He had just sat saddle and looked beyond Buck Wilson, looking at the first barbwire fence to be strung in Burnt Wagon Basin.

'You won't last long,' Gardner had said.

'You aim to run me out?'

Gardner had shrugged; his smile was but a thin line. 'I might, and I might not. This is no farmin' country, fella. Winter's too hard, not enough rain come summer. I'll let the elements run you out. They'll save me the trouble.'

But the next year Buck Wilson's fields had been green and high. And a promoter for the Montana Pacific had come out one day in his buggy and talked Buck into becoming the railroad's land locator in Burnt Wagon.

Buck had said, 'But there'll be trouble with the Rafter Y if we ship in farmers.'

'One man and his cattle can't hold back civilization, Mr. Wilson.'

'Maybe he can't,' Buck had conceded, 'but he sure can do a lot of shootin' before he gives in.'

'My railroad will back you every inch of the way, sir.'

The salary the railroad had offered had not been too big, but it had looked big at that time to Buck Wilson. After his father's death he had shipped out all the scrawny Bar S cattle that had existed through the winter and he had sold the old Bar S buildings to Wade McMahan, who in turn had sold them to Darr Gardner. And Buck had many times found himself thinking he was glad his mother or father had not been alive to see the buildings they had constructed go into Darr Gardner's possession.

The Montana Pacific had also given him a hundred-dollar bonus for each settler, in addition to his salary as land locator. They had sent out a surveyor and he and Buck had run out section lines and township lines. Now the land was clearly defined as to limits, and all he needed was more farmers.

Sometimes he wondered just how far and to what extent the Montana Pacific would help him and his farmers if it came to a showdown with Darr Gardner and Len Huff and the Rafter Y outfit. He had heard of nester-cowman trouble down in Nebraska on the Montana Pacific. The railroad had refused, so he had heard, to send in men to help their farmers—the railroad had not appealed to the courts, either. It had left the hoemen to fight their own fight.

His farmers had come with a little money, but not much—the hard winter had knocked their pocketbooks flat. So flat, in fact, that Buck, on his meager wages, had kept the whole bunch going, more or less. Now every farmer was indebted to him.

One year of good crops, though, and they would have their debts paid off and they would be square with the world. This rain would give them a big boost, Buck thought, playing cards and listening to the rain patter on the roof.

'Your trick, Buck.'

'By gosh, it is.'

Dick Smith winked at Jake Jones. 'He's thinkin' of them two women one of you boys mentioned. Be you thinkin' of Martha Buckman or Laura Fromberg, Buck?'

'Both,' Buck fibbed, dealing.

Buck had been the man who had got Glen Hatfield, the hide and fur buyer, into Burnt Wagon. He had written a big Minneapolis hide outfit and they had sent out Hatfield to buy hides and furs.

The sale of these hides and pelts had been a big boost to his farmers. Even though the sums paid were small, still money was money, and each little bit helped. And every one of his farmers had run a trap line the previous winter.

Buck knew, too, that Darr Gardner had warned Hatfield not to buy from the farmers, for Gardner aimed to run out the hoemen. The sooner they got destitute, the sooner they would leave.

But Glen Hatfield, coming from the city, had apparently paid little heed to the threat of the Rafter Y owner. Apparently he figured that Gardner was, as he put it to Buck, 'just blowing off steam.' But Buck had warned the squat, heavy-set fur buyer that Darr Gardner was dangerous.

'You ain't in Minneapolis now, Hatfield, with a cop on each corner. The closest law is

11

almost a hundred miles away in Chinook, the county seat—an' Chinook's way north of here on the Great Northern.'

'That only happens in books,' Hatfield had said, smiling. 'An' Wild West books, at that.'

Buck had shaken his head slowly. 'Just watch yourself. If any trouble comes, send for me. After all, I'm responsible for gettin' you into Burnt Wagon region.'

'I'm over twenty-one, Buck.'

Glen Hatfield had laughed quietly, seemingly disregarding Buck's warning. Buck had found himself liking this heavy-set, good-natured man. During the week Hatfield had been on this range, Buck had grown to like him very much.

He had shown Hatfield around, and the man had studied the wheat and grain land, even going down and digging into the soil. He had said the soil was very good-looking, very rich-looking.

'Better even than Red River soil, I'd say, Buck.'

'It'll raise anything the climate will allow,' Buck had said enthusiastically. 'All it needs is some rain.'

'Maybe,' Hatfield had said, getting to his feet, 'I might take up a homestead here. I'm tired of dartin' here an' there buyin' furs an' hides.'

12

'Lots of it for homesteadin',' Buck had reminded him.

Jake Jones said, 'Your play, Buck.'

'He's still thinkin' of them heifers,' Dick Smith said. He was a thick, wide man, who walked with a waddling, rolling gait. He weighed close to three hundred, and he had immense strength, despite his fat appearance. He had a homestead on Cottonwood Creek, five miles northwest of Burnt Wagon town. He was a bachelor, not from choice, but he always said, 'No woman would cotton to a mass of lard like me, would they?'

The third farmer was Tim McCarty, a beefy, red-faced Irishman, who had a homestead on Summit Creek. His wife and his four children were in Pennsylvania, waiting for him to get money enough to send for them. He was lonely for them, Buck knew, and he was always willing to show strangers pictures of his wife and children—two boys and two girls.

'Marriage,' said Tim McCarty, 'is a terrible chore.'

Buck said, 'It seems to have treated you well, Tim.'

'Deal,' Dick Smith said. 'Forgit women, please.'

Buck dealt the cards, cigarette smoke trailing upward. He had a swell bunch of

13

farmers, he realized. He cupped his cards and squinted at them, seeing he had a good hand, at last.

He heard the front door of his office open suddenly, then slam. He hollered, 'Back here, fellow.'

The boy was panting. 'Buck, Martha Buckman sent me over. That hide buyer jes' left her store, an' from across the street comes Darr Gardner an' Len Huff, steppin' out of the Cinch Ring Saloon.'

Buck looked up at him. 'Yes, Jackie?'

'It looks like they aim to jump him, Buck!'

Buck threw down his cards, his game forgotten, and he hurried out on the street, followed by his silent farmers and Jackie. Out on the boardwalk he stopped, for he saw they had come too late to stop a fight.

Darr Gardner and Glen Hatfield were already fighting.

CHAPTER TWO

Darr Gardner had a tough reputation as a rough-and-tumble fighter. Once he had whipped an ex-prize fighter down at the county seat. Whipped him and sent him to a hospital. Buck thought, He'll make short

14

work of Glen Hatfield, and that thought was bitter.

The town had come alive. Men, women and kids stood in front of stores and homes and watched the two fighting men. Two dogs broke out fighting in front of the hardware store and this, usually an event in Burnt Wagon town, went by unnoticed, its importance lost against the excitement of two men fighting.

Len Huff stood to one side, and his eyes met those of Buck Wilson. For a moment his derisive, flat eyes studied Buck with cold appraisal. The gunman was calm, his thin face steady. Then Huff looked at the two fighting men, his gaze critical and unhurried.

'By heck,' Jake Jones said, 'Hatfield is whuppin' him, h'ain't he?'

'He's in there,' Dick Smith admitted.

They were right. Hatfield was moving ahead, forcing Darr Gardner back. The hide buyer had shed his coat and it lay on the steps of the Buckman store. His shirt was in shreds, hanging down from his belt. But Buck noticed the roll of fat right above the belt.

That, he decided, would whip Glen Hatfield.

'Gardner's takin' his time,' Tim McCarty said. 'He's waitin' till Glen wears out his wind, an' that won't be long.'

Buck looked back at Huff, but Huff was watching the fighters, who had now moved further out into the street. Beyond Huff he saw Martha Buckman, standing in the doorway of her store.

She saw him and came beside him. 'Buck, stop it, please! Hatfield will get killed!'

Buck said, 'I can't stop it. If I did, they'd fight it out some other time. A fight has to be fought, it seems.'

'Gardner knocked him down, Buck!'

Glen Hatfield was in the mud, standing on all fours. His head was down, and a few feet away, Darr Gardner stood wide-legged, fists up. Gardner was going to have a black eye from this, Buck noticed.

Gardner said, panting, 'Git up an' fight, you hoeman's friend!'

Hatfield did not look up. Buck knew the man was resting. Gardner looked across his opponent and met Buckley Wilson's eyes.

'Maybe I should be givin' this to you 'stead of to this fella, Wilson.'

The whole town heard. The whole town looked at Buck.

Buck said, 'You know where to find me, Gardner.'

Huff smiled, and Buck hated the man's smile. Just then Hatfield came up with a huge uncoiling spring, and he hit Gardner in the

16

mouth. Gardner said, 'All right, fella, this is it,' and they mixed it, the blows loud, the grunts mean and low.

But Hatfield could not stand the pace. This time, when the fur buyer went down, Gardner came in, right foot raised. He aimed to kick Hatfield in the face. But before his boot could find its enemy, a hard hand had grabbed Gardner's right shoulder, sprawling him around.

'Don't do it, you dirty hound!' Buck Wilson's voice was harsh.

For a moment, he and Gardner eyed each other, and he saw the red fire of hate flare in the cowman's eyes. He thought, then, that Gardner would fight him. But then logic came in and claimed Gardner.

Gardner was winded and bloody. Buck was fresh and tough and young. So Gardner said, 'Huff! Len Huff!'

Huff grabbed Buck's arm, and Huff's boots were anchored. Huff's thin, angular face was mean, lighted by a rage to kill. Buck did let go of Gardner then, for the other farmers had moved in between Gardner and Hatfield, making a barrier of flesh and fists that held Gardner back.

Buck pivoted, moving on his hips. Len Huff had hold of his right arm. Buck took his left around, a wicked, fast blow. Huff saw it and tried to duck. He was too slow. The left knocked him back and a townsman held him.

Huff pushed the man back impatiently. Blood formed on the corner of his mouth; his tongue came out with a rapid, licking motion—the blood was gone. He moved ahead one pace, hand on his right hand gun.

Huff asked, 'Where's your gun, farmer?'

Buck said, 'I don't need a gun to whip you.'

Huff looked at him, and the wild rage died. Buck saw sanity creep into those colorless killer-eyes.

Huff said, 'I fight with a gun. Fists are for fools who think strength is great. The man who made a gun made the small fellow as big as the big man.'

Behind Buck, there came the panting voice of Darrell Gardner. 'Don't draw, Len; he ain't got no gun on him.'

'He should pack one.' Huff was stubborn and sure of that point.

Dick Smith and Jake Jones and Tim McCarty had Glen Hatfield on his feet. The fur buyer was groggy and bloody but still, in the core of him, Buck Wilson glimpsed the fighter still present, ready to go back to battle after a second wind.

Buck looked at Huff, but Huff was not dangerous now, for he was clear of anger. The land locator looked at Gardner, saw that the

18

man was not hurt badly, and then he followed the farmers who were propelling Glen Hatfield toward Doc Crow's office, the other side of Buckman's Store.

Martha Buckman said, 'Here's Mr. Hatfield's coat, Buck.'

Buck said, 'Thank you.'

She was a short girl, not much over five feet—her hair was golden and her eyes were as blue as rain-washed skies. Buck and she had grown up together, going to the same school, finding similar likes and dislikes. Then, two years gone, her father had died suddenly, collapsing over his desk, and she had carried on in his store, her mother being kept home by ill health.

'You hit him hard, Buck.'

'Not hard enough, Martha.'

People were moving away. Gardner and Huff were crossing the street, heading for the Rafter Y hangout, the Cinch Ring Saloon. They were alone, with Martha standing on the steps, with Buck holding Hatfield's coat, standing on the plank sidewalk, worn by boots and dragging spurs.

'You hurt his pride more than his body, Buck. You whirled too fast, and he wasn't quite prepared.'

'His way,' Buck reminded her, 'is a gun's way.'

19

'Don't forget that, please.'

'First blood,' Buck Wilson murmured.

Mrs. Martin pushed past them, going into the store, and Martha followed her. Buck went into Doc Crow's office.

They had Glen Hatfield lying on the high cot, with the fat medico bent over him. When Buck Wilson came in Hatfield turned his beaten, bloody head and looked at the door, and Buck saw his sudden smile.

'Howdy, Buckley.'

Buck took the man's skinned hand and held it. 'You should have waited, boy,' he said. 'You took on a big chore right sudden. You don't need to fight my fight, Glen.'

'Your fight! Heck, he jumped on me, Buck. I came out that door and they came across the street, big as the pavement and twice as wide, and the first thing I knew off went my coat, and up went my dukes. Doc, for heck's sake, you've got a man under your hands now, not a work horse!'

'And what a man,' Doc Crow grunted sarcastically.

Buck said, 'He jumped you not because he hated you, but because he wanted to run you out of Burnt Wagon Basin. The few bucks your company has been payin' us broke farmers runs against his grain.'

'He can't run me off, Buck!'

Again Buck Wilson got the sudden feel of this gross man. Hatfield had courage and strength, but above this he had principles. He was strong, then, where Darr Gardner and Len Huff fell down.

Buck said again, 'I'm sorry, Hatfield.'

Hatfield looked at the ceiling, then closed his eyes. His swollen lips showed a big smile. 'Heck, I'm not. Buck, you're fast as light. I thought I could hit fast, but you can move like a bronc kicks. You turned and down Huff went. Good work, kid.'

Buck said, 'You did all right. Where did you learn?'

'Mostly on the streets when I was a youngster. Fought a few semi-pro fights, but I couldn't get to the top, and a man is a fool to be beat up for a few miserable dollars. He's ten years younger than I am.'

Tim McCarty said, in his rich brogue, 'That he is, Mister Hatfield. And that, sir, if I might say it, was what beat you. The years were against you.'

Hatfield said, 'Wonder what kind of a farmer I'd make?'

Buck and his farmers exchanged glances. They knew what the fur buyer was thinking about. His job here was just about through. He had bought all the hides and furs the farmers and the townsmen had. He would

21

leave this town in a few days and behind him would be the hatred held against him by Gardner and Huff.

He would ride out on the coach, thinking of this, thinking that he had gone down, not so much before a man as before the ruthless onslaught of time, and those thoughts, to a man who had pride, would have the acrid taste of vinegar.

'A man never knows what he can do,' Buck said.

Doc Crow said, 'Here, Buck, take hold of this tape. We'll put some on his mug. Tim, hand me those scissors.'

'That I shall do,' Tim McCarty said.

Hatfield seemed talking to himself. 'I can get hold of almost twelve hundred acres on homestead. I could be my own boss. A man never gets any place working for the other fellow. Besides that, each spring I could tour the line, buyin' furs and hides.'

Tim said, 'We'd sure cotton to you, Hatfield.'

'I've got a wife and three kids,' Hatfield said. 'They're back in Minneapolis. A city is no place to raise a couple of boys and a girl. Children need space and they should have horses and dogs.'

Hatfield rolled over. 'Buck, locate me a good claim, eh?'

22

'Any time, Glen.'

'When this horse doctor gets done, we'll ride out, huh?'

'Suits me, Glen.'

Dick Smith said, 'Them Rafter Y men is leavin' town, Buck.'

Buck moved to the fly-specked window and watched Darr Gardner and Len Huff ride out of Burnt Wagon, heading into the rain. When they rode past the medico's office Len Huff glanced at the window and saw Buck watching.

Despite the rain, Buck could see the man's features, and they showed him nothing. The rain came on in a sudden burst, pushing water between them, and Len Huff pulled his head down, his rain-soaked hatbrim hiding his eyes.

Tim McCarty stood beside Buck.

Tim asked, 'Seems odd to me that Darr Gardner would get hisself into a fight, Buck, doesn't it?'

Buck nodded.

'Maybe he figured he'd have to show the town how tough he was, eh?'

'That must've been it,' Buck had to admit.

Glen Hatfield said, 'I figure he thought he had a man he could whip easy. An' he wanted to show Burnt Wagon how tough he was. I

23

guess I didn't make him look any too good, eh?'

'You sure didn't,' Buck returned, smiling a little. Not a pleasant smile, though.

Although none of them said it, each man there was afraid that finally open war had come. Up to now war had been hinted at but none of the fighting had taken place. But possibly the coming of this rain had made the Rafter Y men make their first war-like move.

For many a time Darr Gardner had said, 'Well, this hard winter showed them sodmen what this country is in the wintertime. Some of them danged near froze to death in them sod an' log houses. Now, if we have a dry summer with hot winds an' lots of dust, crops'll sprout an' die, an' them plow pushers'll have to move on, or starve to death.'

But with the coming of this rain, drought was a thing not to be feared for some months, not until late June or July, anyway.

Buck Wilson had made quite a study of wheat, barley and oats—the three main crops his farmers would raise. The Montana Pacific had sent him government circulars and had also sent him circulars that the railroad's agricultural division had compiled.

These head crops, he knew, would need only two good rains a year to make a good stand, providing grasshoppers or hail did not wield out the fields. One rain was needed to provide sufficient moisture right after the seed was planted, or right before. Then another rain would be needed when the plants headed out, so they could form again, full heads of grain.

The one rain had come. The second would be a gamble—in the lap of the gods. But Buck Wilson was not one to worry about a bridge being washed out until he came to that bridge.

He knew, also, that the Rafter Y men had gained much by this fight. Even though he had knocked Len Huff backwards, Huff had lost no prestige. For Len Huff, everybody knew, was a gunman. And who expected a gunman to be efficient with his fists? A gunman's fighting implements were not his fists. He fought with a gun.

Two of his married farmers had their wives with them. Spike Sherman, who had built his sod shack on Wild Horse Flat, was only twenty-one, but he had his wife, Shannon, and baby girl, Elsa, with him. Jack Lacey, who had his claim next to Buck's, also had his wife on his homestead, and Frances Lacey would be afraid for her husband's safety, when she heard about this fight on Burnt Wagon's muddy main street.

Shannon Sherman, too, would fear for her husband's safety. Buck gave Spike Sherman and Jack Lacey a moment's thought, then decided to let time tell him how useful these men would be, for he figured they would have to move in direct opposition to the wishes of their wives. And it wasn't too easy for a man to disregard the wishes of a woman he loved.

Doc Crow said, 'That'll be all, Mr. Hatfield.'

Glen Hatfield sat up and looked at himself in the hand mirror Doc Crow had handed him. He inspected his face, tilting his head, and then he smiled widely.

'Look almost like a mummy.'

'Not quite that good-looking,' Buck Wilson joked.

CHAPTER THREE

Buck got Glen Hatfield to his room in the Burnt Wagon House, then came into the lobby again, fully aware of the proprietor's far from cordial gaze.

The owner was an old, broken-down cowman who had run cattle in Wyoming, then had sold out and, a few years before, had bought the Burnt Wagon House. Therefore his sympathies, Buck knew, were all with the Rafter Y.

'That fella got a nurse?' the old cowpoke demanded.

Buck said quietly, 'He's all right. He doesn't need a nurse. Doc gave him a sedative and he'll look in about nine tonight, he said.'

'What's a sedative?' suspiciously.

Buck said, 'Look it up in the dictionary,' and stepped out into a world that consisted of swirling rain.

The whist game forgotten, the three farmers were mounting their broncs, and they held in their mounts as Buck came along the sidewalk, bent against the wind's push.

Tim McCarty said, 'Us for our homes, Buck.'

Buck said, 'A cold ride, Tim.'

'Now if I had me ol' woman here from Pennsylvania,' Tim McCarty said, 'it would be a good bowl of hot soup I would have a-waitin' me as I rid into the yard.'

Jake Jones said, 'Buck, we should have a meeting, and talk this over. Your place is the biggest.'

'Tomorrow night?' Buck asked.

They exchanged glances, seeming to find no dissension.

'I'll tell Spike Sherman and Horace Browning,' Tim said. 'I'll ride over to their farms this evenin' yet.'

'I'll tell Jack Lacey,' Jake Jones said.

'Tomorrow evening, then,' Buck confirmed.

They all nodded, very seriously. Then they turned their horses and rode into the rain, hunched over in wet saddles, horses plodding because of the uncertain footing.

'Hello, Buck.'

The voice was feminine, and it fit Laura Fromberg. She was dark, this girl—she was twenty, and her face was sweet and innocent.

Buck asked, 'School out already?'

'Yep, and for the week, too.'

'That's right, it is Friday.' Buck took her books. 'Got an apple you want me to carry, too, teacher?'

She sighed and hooked her arm in his. 'Buck, you'd joke with the devil ready to stick you with a hot pitchfork. I heard about the fight, even at school; I'm afraid.'

'I'm not.'

She looked up at him, her dark eyes round. 'You're not?'

Buck said, 'When it comes, it comes.'

'Fatalist?'

'Yes, I guess so.'

When they went past Buckman's store, Buck glanced through the big front windows. Martha Buckman was behind the counter selling something to a townswoman. She looked up, saw them, met Buck's eyes. Buck

28

saw her bite her bottom lip and look hurriedly back at her customer.

He remembered Smitty saying, 'Heck, he's got two women after him right now,' and he remembered how the whist players had laughed at Dick Smith's remark.

But maybe these two women were chasing him.

For some reason that thought was a little alarming. He had been so busy getting his own claim in order and getting his farmers located that he had not had much time to think about any woman, even Martha Buckman or Laura Fromberg.

Now he found himself comparing the two. And he had to admit to himself that Laura Fromberg was the more fascinating. He sought to find a reason for this.

He realized he had known Laura only a few months. She had come at Christmas time from Denver to take over the local grammar school, for the original teacher had been called home to the East due to illness in her family.

And he had known Martha Buckman as long as he could remember. He had known her father well and he still thought a lot of Mrs. Buckman, who had turned the store over entirely to the hands of Martha, her only child.

Maybe, because he had known Martha for

so long, their acquaintanceship had worn thin the glamour Martha would have possessed had he just met her, if such a thing were possible. And it was not.

Martha was lithe and small, still the tomboy. She could lope across the prairie, sitting her horse like a Sioux Indian, her blonde hair whipping back, her blue eyes aglow and sparkling.

Lately he had found himself glancing at Martha much more often than he used to. Overnight she seemed to have turned into a young woman, her girlhood falling from her. But he knew this was not true.

She had not suddenly matured. He had, for the first time, just noticed her womanly maturity. She was slow-spoken, slow to anger, but once she became angered, she was a wildcat.

Grammar school days had taught him that.

Laura was Martha's opposite. Martha was light complexioned, whereas Laura was dark, mysterious. She was always neat and trim, but sometimes her sharpness disturbed Buck Wilson.

He blamed this sharpness upon her teaching job.

He had a hunch the first teacher had not left due to illness in her family. For nobody in Burnt Wagon had ever heard her mention her family until the day she suddenly resigned.

Buck figured she had left because the Burnt Wagon kids had been too hard to handle. But from what he had heard, Laura handled the tough kids all right.

Maybe the tension of her work sometimes made her sharp-tongued.

She and Buck had attended a few of the local dances together, for sometimes Martha had to keep her store open until almost midnight on Saturdays, the day of the dances, and the day when the farmers came to town for groceries.

Laura had also attended a few social affairs with Darr Gardner. One time she had even turned down Buck's offer to go to a dance with the big Rafter Y owner. That had been about two months ago.

Since that dance, she had never been seen with Gardner again.

Buck had wondered a number of times if she and the arrogant Rafter Y owner had quarreled. But he had never asked her for details. He was not engaged to her, nor was he engaged to Martha, either.

She stopped by the gate. 'Well, Buck, what do you say?'

He knew what she meant, but he played ignorant. 'Say about what, Laura?'

'About the Rafter Y and your farmers, of

course.'

He detected the sharpness in her voice.

He said, 'We're meeting tomorrow night. From what I gather, we won't move against the Rafter Y. If there is a war, then the Rafter Y has to start it. We're all law-abiding citizens trying to make an honest living.'

'But your fences are cutting in on Rafter Y grass, pushing Gardner's cattle back into the hills for summer range. Winters he used to graze on land you now have under fence.'

Buckley Wilson pointed out that Gardner had not had deeds or patents to the land on which he had run cattle. He had claimed ownership through the *squatters' right* theory, for he had bought from Wade McMahan, who had *squatted* on this range.

'The squatters' right theory has been called illegal by about three territorial courts that I know of. Uncle Sam refuses to recognize ownership claimed under that theory.'

'Oh, I see.'

Buck went on with, 'When me an' my farmers have spent a year on our land, then we get our deeds. Uncle Sam signs them, and his signature is good enough for me, believe you me. I get my deed next week, but my farmers have to wait until their homestead papers are filed and they've put a year in on their homesteads.'

'Gardner knows that, doesn't he?'

'Sure, he knows it. He jest doesn't want to recognize it. Well, here we are at Standifer's gate. I'd go in with you, but the old girl will holler, as usual. So good-bye.'

'Tomorrow is the dance at the schoolhouse, Buck. My pupils decorated the building all afternoon.'

Buck smiled. 'I won't be there. Out to my farm at the meeting. Reckon you'll have to lean on Darr Gardner's arm, Laura.'

She stuck out her tongue at him, then ran up the walk to the house. Buck returned to his office, where he sat down in the dusk and moodily regarded his muddy boots.

When he had filed on his homestead, he had filed on a piece of land where Wade McMahan had first built his ranch house. McMahan had abandoned this site in a few years and moved his headquarters to the present location of the Rafter Y, ten miles out of town on Cow Creek.

After McMahan had sold to Darr Gardner, Gardner had used the old ranch house as a line camp. Then Buck had filed homestead papers on the quarter section of land that held the ranch house and the buildings that McMahan had abandoned.

Thus he had become owner of the house and buildings by merely filing on the ground on which they stood.

33 *ltd*

Gardner had gone to the county seat and consulted a government attorney, who proved to him that when a man filed a homestead, everything above ground went with the land, for if the land had no title, then surely the property on it was without an owner, also.

Gardner had had to swallow it.

The Rafter Y had other line camps, although none of them had a building as big as the old ranch house. Those that were in the basin were immediately claimed by Gardner, who hurriedly had cowpunchers file on them as homesteads. But his prize line camp was out of his grasp.

Buckley Wilson was living in it. Wilson was using corrals he had built, sheds and barns he had kept in repair.

Although Darr Gardner had never jumped Buck about the buildings, Buck Wilson knew that the owner of the Rafter Y held a deep, personal hatred toward him. More than the value of the buildings involved was at stake.

Buck had outwitted and outthought the cowman. And Darr Gardner had his pride— and a deep, stubborn pride it was.

Buck got out of his chair and went to the Broken Spur Café, where he ate his supper. Wong Ling, the Chinese owner, usually kept up a running chatter, but tonight he was strangely silent. Business was dull and Buck heard him talking Chinese to his stove, and he gathered, from the man's strong tone, that he was swearing.

'What's the matter, Wong?'

'Allee time the trouble, Buckley boy. Allee time the trouble.' He peered at Buck with sharp brown eyes. 'You thinkee you win?'

'We gotta win, Wong.'

'No win allee time. Man gotta lose somee time.'

Buck nodded.

'That Chinese boy—he out to your farm?'

'You mean Hatchet Joe?'

'That him. He out there?'

Buck told the cook that Hatchet Joe was out at the farm.

'He good boy?'

'Good cook. Heck, he used to cook for my dad, when he was in the cow business. You were here then, Wong.'

'Me forgot. I no mean him good cook.'

They were alone in the café. Buck looked inquiringly over a forkful of egg. His brows lifted and formed a question.

'What do you mean, Wong?'

'Him good rifle shot, no?'

Buck saw what the Chinese was driving at. Wong Ling was warning him that Darr Gardner and Len Huff would hit back at him and his farmers. This knowledge, of course, was not new to Buck. Still, he felt good—another human being was worried about him.

He had known Wong Ling all his life. When he and his dad and mother had come into town years ago from the ranch—and it seemed years and years and years back—they had always eaten at Wong Ling's café.

And Wong had always had a little candy or some other present for him.

Buck found his own face very serious. Then he said, 'Wong, a man has to fight sometimes, doesn't he?'

'Yes, sometime, he hafta fight.'

'When?'

Wong Ling scratched his chin. 'When he fight for his rights, he have to fight. Only time worth fightin', Buckley.'

Buck said, 'That's what us farmers think, Wong Ling.'

'Then you win.'

That seemed settled. Wong Ling went back to his kitchen. This time, he sang to his stove.

Buck finished eating, paid his bill, then went outside. Night had come and Martha Buckman was locking the door on her store.

Buck said, 'Another day, another dollar.'

'Oh, I didn't see you coming, Buck!'

Buck walked home with her. She chatted about her work, her mother, but Buck figured the chatter was a camouflage. She was worried

36

about the trouble that was stalking across this range. Buck Wilson got this impression, and it registered on him, and he thought he detected worry about his safety in it.

Her mother was the same, not well, not really sick. Buck saw she had quite a load to carry but she was carrying it on square shoulders. They came to her home, the rain making its welcome sounds.

'Won't you come in, Buckley?'

He said, 'Your mother might be asleep and I would not want to wake her. And I'd best look in on Glen Hatfield before I go to bed. Furthermore, you've had a busy day.'

She sighed, 'I'm tired, and tomorrow night is my busy night, too.'

She seemed loath to go into the house. Buck seemed to have no desire to be on his way. She looked up at him, and he thought: Gosh, she's small. He wanted to protect her and take care of her suddenly.

The feeling came out of nowhere, and held him.

'See anybody on the street?'

She looked up and down the dark, rain-filled street with its huge cottonwood and poplar trees.

'Why, no. Why did you ask?'

Buck had his arm around her, and he kissed her on the lips. It was a rough, clumsy kiss, he

37

realized. He had never kissed her before. He was a little flustered when he straightened.

'Why, Buck . . .'

'Good night, Martha.'

'Good night!'

She turned and ran up the gravel walk. Buck thought: I sure bungled that, and watched until she entered. Light came out when the door opened, flashed across wet shrubs and the walk, then was cut short by the closing of the door.

Buck walked back toward town.

Now what did she think of him after he had fallen victim to his sudden whim? Had her *good night* been as abrupt as it sounded? Sometimes, Buckley Wilson, you sure do foolish things, he thought.

Oh, shucks, if she is mad, she'll forget it in a little while.

Because it was a weekday night, the street was deserted. Not a horse or rig was at a hitchrack, not a dog slunk through the night. With this rain falling all night, the soil would store up a lot of moisture by morning.

There was a light in Doc Crow's office and Buck knocked. Doc Crow called, 'Come in,' and when Buck entered the room the portly medico was slipping into his yellow slicker.

'How's Hatfield?'

Doc Crow said, 'I was just going to the hotel

38

before I turned in. Come along, Buck.'

They walked down the street toward the Burnt Wagon House, both silent. Doc's overshoes splashed in the pools of water. They crossed the empty lobby and went to Hatfield's room. A slim ribbon of light lay under the door and they entered without knocking.

Hatfield's head swiveled, looked at them. Doc sat down beside the injured man, but Buck stood, Stetson in hand.

Hatfield looked up at Buck, and the fur buyer's eyes were too bright. His face—what you could see of it through the bandages—was also too bright, Buck thought. Fever lighted it with its hot torch.

Doc Crow dropped Hatfield's wrist.

'Uh-huh,' the medico said. 'How do you feel?'

Hatfield's tongue wet his cracked bottom lip. 'Rough, Doc.'

Doc Crow glanced at the pitcher of water that had been full when he had left that afternoon. Now it was empty. The glass beside it was empty too.

Glen Hatfield closed his eyes.

Doc Crow made a motion with his head, and Buck went out the door ahead of him. They got out of hearing distance from the sick man and the medico told Buck that Hatfield

39

had a very fast pulse and a high fever.

'What causes that, Doc?'

The medico thought that perhaps one of Darr Gardner's blows to the belly had hurt the fur buyer more than they had thought.

'He might be bleeding a little internally. I'm moving in a cot and staying beside him tonight.'

Buck Wilson felt very helpless. He had the helpless feeling that comes to a layman when he is in the presence of a friend who is very sick—a friend he cannot help because he knows nothing about medicine.

'Anything I can do, Doc?'

'Not now, Buck.'

Without asking the proprietor's permission, they searched the empty rooms until they found an old army cot and they carried it, blankets and all, into Glen Hatfield's room.

Hatfield looked at them, said nothing, then closed his eyes again.

Buck left Doc Crow sitting on the cot.

The land locator went to his office and undressed in the dark, sitting on his bed and thinking. He had difficulty getting to sleep. His last thought was that if Glen Hatfield died, he would then kill Darrell Gardner.

But Hatfield *couldn't* die.

CHAPTER FOUR

Gardner said, 'Well, that boy learned a lesson.'

Len Huff leaned forward, for the rain had been too noisy. He asked, 'What did you say, Darr?'

Gardner scowled, but repeated the statement.

Huff leaned back in saddle, hands on his saddlehorn. 'He sure did learn that,' he concurred.

Gardner said, looking into the rain, 'Darn this rain, anyway.'

Huff said nothing, head deep in the collar of his oilskin slicker. He was remembering a rain-washed street and a man whirling unexpectedly. He touched his lips with his tongue and found them swollen slightly. He was a vain man, a small man, both in stature and in pride. The touch of his swollen lips was acid to his tongue, making him angry and tough.

Gardner stood on stirrups and looked across rain-filled Burnt Wagon Basin. The land stretched out, flat and level, marked by the winding course of the creeks, marked by the cottonwoods and box-elders around and along

41

these creeks. The land moved out, and rain hid it, hiding it from his eyes.

'A desolate land,' Huff said.

Gardner said, 'A cowman always lives on the edge of desolation. If his land is good he loses it to civilization. They come in, they do, and they farm it, and a farm pays better than cattle.'

'Then let's go farming.'

Was that cynicism in Len Huff's tone?

Gardner said stoutly, 'This is not farming land.'

'They're farming it.'

'They're *trying* to farm it,' Darr Gardner corrected him.

Huff shrugged. Frankly, he did not want farmers in Burnt Wagon Basin for only one reason. If the farmers stayed, more farmers would come, and the arrival of each farmer could cut deeper into Rafter Y range. And if the Rafter Y fell, he would lose a good job—a job that paid him twice the wages a similar job would provide any other place.

It had started out as that—just a job, a good job. But now, it was beyond the point of mere wages. When Buckley Wilson had whirled and had pounded him backwards, then the wages had fallen into the background, and hate had pushed them there. It had gone beyond the mere sum of dollars and cents.

42

That blow, coming unexpectedly, had made this thing larger, bringing in the element of pride. For, at his core, this man Len Huff, above all, was a proud man; he had the sullen, deep pride of the small man.

Because of his small physical stature, he had developed his precision with a pistol. What he could not win through muscles he would win through speed and power with a six-gun.

Because of this prowess, men had walked around him and avoided trouble, and this had been caviar to his ego. But today, Buck Wilson had hit him, driving him back, and Buck Wilson had not had a gun on him.

He knew that Buck could whip him with fists. But with a gun, he was Buck's master. And some day, he vowed, this would be finished with a gun. He was not thinking of his soft job and the soft wages it paid.

He was thinking of revenge.

He glanced at his boss. Now Darr Gardner had sunk deep between horn and cantle, a heavy man riding a big gelding. And Len Huff thought, I wonder what he's thinkin' about? but he made no effort to find out.

Gardner, he knew, would not tell him, even if he did ask. But he was not going to ask, for he knew what his answer, if any, would be.

The rain had switched directions, and now it came from behind them.

43

Gardner reached up and touched his left eye and decided it would be black inside of a few hours.

Huff saw the gesture and turned away, for Gardner was looking at him. Huff kept his face straight; Gardner looked the other way.

The tie between them was not based on friendship. Of course, they were friends, but friends only because of a monetary relationship. Each needed the other. That was the basis of their friendship, if it could be called such.

Huff needed Gardner because Gardner was the big man, the boss, of Burnt Wagon Basin. He was the man who could pay the high wages. And Gardner needed Huff because of Huff's .45, and the thin man's speed with that .45.

There it was—simple, elementary.

Actually, Huff felt ridicule toward Darr Gardner. In his estimation, Gardner was a blunderer. His intelligence was not deep. And Len Huff knew this estimation was a false one, yet he found solace in it. Gardner, he knew, was smart enough; Gardner did not blunder.

Gardner had walked out on Burnt Wagon's main street and called Glen Hatfield. Gardner could have taken one of his cowboys into town, fired him with a few drinks, and then

Gardner could have said, 'Here's five bucks, fellow. Go out and beat that fur buyer to the mud. When you come back, there's another five waiting for you.'

It could have been that simple.

But, no! Gardner had gone out himself, for he wanted to show this town, and especially those farmers, that he could handle his own fists. And Gardner had whipped Glen Hatfield. Gardner, himself, had driven Hatfield down into the mud, there on that rain-driven street.

Gardner had made no blunder.

Word would get around now. In fact, it was going through the basin at this moment, being repeated and repeated. Darr Gardner had whipped the fur buyer. He had walked out, big and tough, and he had sent Glen Hatfield into the mud, bloody and beaten.

He had whipped Hatfield, not so much because he had hated the man, but for the main purpose of showing the farmers he was not going to lose his range sitting down. The fight had, in reality, been a warning for the farmers.

Huff asked, 'Well, what's next, Darr?'

Gardner looked at him, his face blank. He studied his foreman with an almost open insolence.

'No use rushin' our cards, Len.'

45

Huff said, 'We should hit while the iron is hot. Pile one thing onto the top of the other, an' together they mean more to these farmers.'

Gardner nodded, looked back at the muddy road. They were riding down a lane that had not been here the year before. On each side barbwire stretched, solid and taut, held by diamond-willow posts.

A year ago, a man didn't have to ride through a lane to get to the big Rafter Y. He could cut across country as the crow flies and he'd never pass through a lane or open a gate. But here it was—a shiny, brittle barbwire fence, forcing them to ride around it. Gardner felt his rage well up inside of him as he rode.

It was Spike Sherman's fence, Darr Gardner knew. Young Sherman had almost a section under fence—good grass on which Rafter Y cows had grazed for years. But they weren't grazing there now.

This rubbed against Darr Gardner, driving a black vein into his thoughts. He looked back at the hills, for Spike Sherman had built his log house back there. He could not see the house and the barn, for the rain was a muddy thickness and dust was rapidly sifting through it to add more darkness.

Len Huff breathed, 'One of the farmers, along the fence ahead of us . . .'

'Sherman,' Gardner said.

Spike Sherman was walking toward them, inside his fence and along the border of his grain field. The wheat had been seeded early and was about two inches high. The loose ground of his field was really soaking in the rain.

Gardner said, 'Here's a gate.'

Len Huff looked at him, a question in his bland eyes. Gardner had no reason to be leaning down from saddle and loosening the latch of the barbwire gate. Then Huff realized Gardner aimed to ride across the wheat field, taking a short-cut to the Rafter Y.

Gardner threw the gate back, straightening in leather.

'Here he comes,' Len Huff said. 'On the run, too.'

Sherman came running, despite the mud. He hollered, 'Hey, you two, stay off'n my field!'

Huff glanced toward the location of Spike Sherman's house, but the rain hid it. Gardner rode out into the field about ten feet, then stopped as Spike Sherman came up, breathing hard from his run in the mud.

Sherman said, 'Get outa that field! Ride aroun' by the fence, the way you're supposed to ride! You cain't tromp down my wheat stand!'

Gardner said, 'We pay attention to no

fences, Sherman.'

Sherman stood on wide legs, looking up at Gardner. Hate was in his eyes, metallic and hard. He was young and without guile, for the few years had not yet added subtleness to his character. Yet, despite his anger, he seemed suddenly to become very suspicious.

'What happened to your face, Gardner?'

'Hatfield and me mixed.'

Spike Sherman looked at Huff.

Huff said, 'No, Hatfield ain't dead. But he will be, if he mixes up with the Rafter Y again.'

Sherman said, 'You're trying to pull me into trouble, you are.' He stepped back, and Huff was behind him.

Huff leaned on his left stirrup. His .45 rose once and then chopped down in a vicious arc. The barrel smashed through Spike Sherman's rain helmet and set the farmer lurching ahead.

Huff leaned forward further, gun rising. Sherman was out of reach. Huff said to Gardner, 'Get him, Darr.'

Len Huff's voice did not rise.

Gardner kicked his right foot out of the oxbow stirrup. Sherman was stunned, almost out on his feet. Gardner kicked him viciously. His boot landed on Spike Sherman's jaw.

Huff watched Gardner's face as the Rafter Y man kicked again. Gardner's face was

48

black, colored with rage, and Huff thought it was a killer's face. He wondered why Gardner would let his emotion show.

His own face was bland, without life.

Huff heard the savage, crushing smash of Gardner's boot, which made itself heard even above the rain. The boot came back, red with blood, and then Huff looked at Sherman, who lay on his side in the plowed earth.

Huff said, 'He'll remember that, Gardner.'

Gardner sucked in air, and the blackness left him. His eyes pulled down, crafty and mean, and he weighed this in his mind. Huff watched him and saw his conjecture, and below them Spike Sherman moaned. Huff looked down at Sherman, marked him as unconscious for some time, then looked back at the Rafter Y owner.

'We'd best ride,' Huff said.

Gardner snarled, 'Afraid, Len?'

Huff shrugged his shoulders delicately. 'His wife might have seen. I don't want a .30–30 slug between my shoulders.'

'She never saw,' Gardner said, his voice surly.

Huff sent him a slanting glance. 'Don't jump on me, Gardner. You might find me a hard one to beat to the earth.'

Gardner looked at him, smiling thinly. 'Come on,' he said, turning his horse.

49

They rode at a walk, Gardner a pace ahead of Huff. Their horses plodded through the loose wet earth. When their hoofs came up the wheat plants came up, also. When their hoofs sank down they buried the fresh young plants in the mud.

Gardner said, 'These tracks will be across this field even when it is ripe for the binder.'

'If it gets ripe.'

Gardner's eyes asked a question.

Huff said quietly, 'Ripe wheat will burn good with any kind of wind. Doesn't need much wind, either.'

'These farmers won't harvest their crops,' Gardner stated. 'My cattle will eat these head crops down.'

Huff glanced toward the location of Sherman's house. Gardner caught the glance and said, 'You can't see his shack, can you?' He did not wait for an answer. 'Then she can't see us.'

'She has a baby girl,' Huff said slowly. 'I saw the child down in town one day. Her name is Elsa.'

Darr Gardner gave his foreman a surprised look.

'Purty little girl,' Huff said.

Gardner looked ahead, silent. They came to the fence on the opposite side of the field. There was no gate here, so they made one with

50

the wire nippers that Gardner carried tied to his saddle.

They rode through the cut fence, and the hard earth of the prairie was under their broncs' shod hoofs. Gardner used his spurs and his horse headed into a lope, with Huff riding close at his flank.

They went past Rafter Y cattle, standing bunched under trees along the creeks, humped for protection under the rims of the coulees. They skirted the cottonwoods on Cow Creek, and Huff said, 'Ford will be high.'

'Not too high, Huff.'

'Swim a bronc.'

'Bet?'

'Five bucks.'

They hit the ford, the night on them. Huff collected on the opposite side. He ran his forefinger around the gold piece, judged it to be the correct size, and put it in his watch pocket.

They loped into the Rafter Y ranch within five minutes. A guard was in the cottonwoods and, although he could not see the man, Darr Gardner hollered out, 'Burnt Wagon.'

A voice came back, 'Burnt Wagon.'

They rode into the barn. It had the smell of manure and warm horseflesh. It broke the wind and held warmth. They went down with creaking gear and the hostler came out of his room at the far end of the long building.

'Rough night, men.'

Huff looked at the gold piece.

'You don't trust a man, eh?'

Huff lifted his level eyes to his boss. 'Heck, no,' he said. 'I trust nobody but a gent named Len Huff.'

The hostler was peeling saddles off their wet mounts. He kept glancing at Gardner, and the Rafter Y man knew he was wondering about his black eye.

Gardner let him wonder.

Huff said, 'Me for my bed,' and he and Gardner left the protection of the barn, bent against the rain. Huff turned off without a word, going to his foreman shack, set across from the bunkhouse. Gardner noticed lights in the bunkhouse, but he did not look in on his riders.

He went to the darkened, rain-pounded ranch house.

CHAPTER FIVE

The sound came, breaking through the darkness of sleep, and finally it made an impression on Buckley Wilson. His mind pushed it aside, but the sound kept pestering him, and finally he realized somebody was knocking at the door.

'That you, Hatchet Joe?'

'No, this is Mrs. Sherman.'

Buck was wide awake now. 'Just a minute, until I dress.' He lit the lamp, all vestiges of sleep quickly departing. Now what did Mrs. Sherman want at this hour? He looked at the clock. He had been asleep only a few minutes.

He was wearing his dressing-robe and his slippers when he admitted the slicker-draped, worried young housewife.

'What—what is it, madam?'

Words tumbled from her cold lips. Her husband had been beaten by Darr Gardner and Len Huff, who had run their broncs across their wheat field, and had cut their fence.

Buck sat on the bed, a cold hand wrapping itself around his guts.

'When did this happen?'

'Just about dusk, Buck.'

Buck asked, 'Why didn't you come in and tell me before?'

Her husband had come staggering home, and had told his grisly story. She had put him to bed and doctored him as best she could.

'Spike didn't want me to go in and tell you. He said he wasn't seriously hurt, and there was no need to bother you. So I waited until he was asleep, and then I hooked up a team and drove in, for I want Doc Crow to look at him.'

'Doc Crow is down in his office, I guess. He sleeps there.' Memory washed through Buck's sleepy mind. 'No, he's up at the hotel, with Glen Hatfield.'

'I tried his office, but he wasn't there.'

Buck said, 'Step outside a moment, and I'll go with you.'

'The rain seems to be stopping.'

She went outside, and Buck hurriedly dressed, slipping into his slicker as he shut the door. Mrs. Sherman was right. The sky was clearing to the west, and the clouds overhead were thinning. The wind had gathered strength, sweeping the clouds to the east, and it had a touch of chill.

Buck and the housewife hurried across town, both silent. Buck wondered if there was anything he could do about the beating of Spike Sherman. Yes, and the Rafter Y men had ridden across his wet field, and had cut his three wire fence.

But what could he do?

With the sheriff one hundred miles away, up at Chinook on Milk River ... Of course, he could wire out of the Montana Pacific's depot, here in Burnt Wagon, and the wire

54

would reach Chinook via the Great Northern's telegraph. But would the sheriff pay any attention to the call?

Buck doubted if the crusty old cowman, who was now sheriff, would even send over a deputy. For the sheriff, he knew, was in sympathy with the cowmen. He had shown that when the cowmen had run the nesters out of that section of Milk River Valley. But still he would notify the lawmen.

'I'll call the sheriff over,' he told Mrs. Sherman.

'Spike says the sheriff won't come.'

'We'll go on record as calling him, whether he comes or not. If this does get into court, then, our skirts will be clear.'

'Well, yes.'

Buck caught the edge of her worry. She was a city woman, a woman not used to this violence. She was afraid for her man and her home. Actually, she was, in her unknowing way, an enemy to Buck's purpose. She would be afraid from now on, and this fear, of course, would influence her husband.

'Darr Gardner kicked Spike.'

Buck said, 'He'll get his, Mrs. Sherman.'

Buck knew what would stop this war. A .45 slug accurately placed in the brisket of one Darrell Gardner. But he did not mention this to the woman. He could see no percentage in

55

placing additional fears on her shoulders.

He realized this thing had come to a sudden head. For months it had been simmering on the back of the stove; now it was directly over the fire. The rain was the cause of it, he figured.

Had the spring continued without rain, the Rafter Y would have won its battle without firing a gun. For drought would have broken Buck and his six farmers. But the rain had come and had saved them, at least temporarily.

He didn't know just how to strike back at Darr Gardner and Len Huff. He was no gunman, nor were his farmers gunmen. Huff could handle a gun, and other riders on the big Rafter Y were also gun throwers. Yes, and Gardner himself was no slouch with a pistol or rifle.

They crossed the lobby, which was deserted. A kerosene lamp, the wick turned low, stood on the counter. Beside it was a nickel-plated hand bell.

'Which room?' Mrs. Sherman asked.

Buck said, 'Follow me.' They went down the corridor, the lamp behind them throwing grotesque shadows ahead of them, and Buck knocked on the door of Glen Hatfield's room.

'Oh, Doc.'

Doc Crow was a light sleeper. Buck heard

56

the cot move; then a voice asked, 'Who is there?'

'Buck Wilson.'

'The door is unlocked, Buck.'

They stepped into the warm, closed room. Darkness seemed to reach out and grab them, wrapping its cloak around them.

Doc Crow said softly, 'Hatfield is asleep.'

Buck told him, 'Mrs. Sherman is with me.' But the medico already had the lamp lighted. He wore a long woolen nightgown and a red night cap was on his head.

'Excuse my appearance, madam, please. But what brought you into town on such a wild night? The rain's coming down by the bucketful.'

She told him about her husband's trouble. Buck watched the medico's heavy face, saw the frown creep into it.

'So the trouble has really started.'

Nobody answered. Doc Crow seemed to be talking to himself.

'Go down and harness my team, Buck, and hitch them to my buggy.'

Buck was looking down at Glen Hatfield. The man was asleep, flat on his back. His nostrils dilated and moved, and his snoring was light. The land locator's eyes asked the medico a question.

'Under a sedative, Buck.'

'Leave him alone, Doc?' Buck asked.

'I'll get Mrs. Myers out of bed,' Doc Crow said. 'Now, if you'll go with Buck, Mrs. Sherman, while I dress . . .'

Buck and the housewife went to the barn behind Doc Crow's office. The land locator lighted the lantern and the team looked at him from the stalls, eyes wide in the yellow light.

Buck harnessed the horses, led them outside, and hitched them to the buggy. He got the side curtains and windshield from the barn and installed them on the rig, with Mrs. Sherman helping him.

'Here comes Doc, Buck.'

Doc said, 'You drive, Buck.'

They got Mrs. Sherman between them and the three crowded into the seat. Buck could feel the trembling of the woman's cold body as he gigged the team down the main street and drew in his lines before Mrs. Myers' home.

Doc said, 'I'll go in.'

Buck and Mrs. Sherman were silent as they sat in the buggy. The rain was thinning down, making less noise against the celluloid windshield. Finally the doctor and Mrs. Myers came out on the porch, the lamplight behind them illuminating them clearly.

'I'll go right to the hotel, Doctor Crow.'

Buck heard the doctor thank her, and then the buggy sagged as the obese man climbed in.

58

They headed out of town, with Buck driving the team as if he owned them, but never getting them above a trot.

The going was too slippery. If a bronc slipped and fell at a fast pace, the buggy might run over him and break up.

Mrs. Sherman said, 'Mr. Hatfield did not look too well, or so it seemed to me. I've done practical nursing.'

Doc Crow grunted something. Buck could not make out what the medico had said, for the wheels slopped and sucked the mud, and the rain still made a fine noise.

Doc asked, 'And do you think your husband has any broken bones?'

Mrs. Sherman thought her husband's jaw was broken. She wasn't sure, but she thought a kick had broken his jaw.

Doc said, 'We'll soon find out.'

'Where's Elsa?' Buck asked.

Her little daughter was home in bed and, she hoped, sound asleep. From then on to the ranch, the trio was silent. Buck nursed his thoughts and found them far from agreeable.

Mrs. Sherman had left her team and rig in Doc Crow's barn. Buck had said he would drive the outfit out in the morning, right after he had wired the sheriff over in Chinook.

It was about five miles to the Sherman farm. But to Buck it seemed endless miles, for each thought of young Spike Sherman made the road seem even slower to traverse. He liked the young farmer.

Heck, Spike wasn't any more than a big kid. He thought the world of his young wife, and little Elsa was the greatest baby in the world.

'Well,' said Doc Crow, 'here we are.' He looked up at the sky. 'And our rain is almost a thing of the past.'

'We've had enough for now,' Buck said. 'No use gettin' it all at once.'

Mrs. Sherman had left a lamp burning in the front room. She picked it up and carried it to the bedroom. When she entered, the light awakened her husband.

'What's goin' on, Shannon?'

'I went in town for the doctor.'

'Why, dang it, no need to get doc out on a night like this.' Spike Sherman tried to get his weight on his elbow but failed.

'My job, young man,' Doc said, sitting down in the chair beside the bed.

From the other room came the sounds of Elsa. Buck and Mrs. Sherman went into the room. The child was sitting up in her crib, watching them.

'Good girl,' Buck said. 'She looks like she's been awake for some time, too. Yet she didn't cry.'

Mrs. Sherman kissed her girl and laid her back on the pillow. 'Now go to sleep, honey.'

Elsa kept eyeing Buck, knowing he was a stranger. The homeliness of the scene struck the land locator with a blow of pity for this woman and this child. He only hoped nothing was serious with Spike.

He went into the other bedroom, leaving the mother and child alone. Doc Crow was digging in his bag for something.

'How's the jaw?' Buck asked Spike.

Spike rubbed it gingerly. 'Sore, but no bones broken. Reckon somebody really must have kicked me. I went out like a lantern caught in a cyclone. I should have known better than to let that rat of a Len Huff swing in behind me.'

'Hard to watch two men at once,' Buck admitted.

Sherman lay back, hands laced behind his head. 'I'll get them two sons if it's the last thing I do on this earth.' He looked at Buck. 'What do you think about Shannon?'

'She's afraid.'

'She mention we should leave?'

'No.'

Doc Crow said, 'Buck, get me a glass of water, please?'

Buck went to the kichen and dippered a glass of water out of the pail and returned with

61

it. Doc Crow dropped some powders in it and these colored the water to a milkish-white.

'Drink this, Spike.'

Spike drank it hurriedly, and handed the glass back, his face showing his distaste. 'Doc, they teach you guys in colleges how to make our lives miserable, I reckon.'

'I learned mine firsthand,' Doc Crow said, his face straight. Buck caught his wink, but Spike Sherman did not see it.

Spike Sherman worked his lips, still tasting the bitterness of the potion. He swallowed, cleared his throat.

'Well, I can tell you this, Buck, and I mean it: I'm not running from this homestead, not for Darr Gardner or Len Huff, or anybody that looks like either of them. Once I might have left, but not now.'

Doc buttoned down his bag.

Buckley Wilson nodded, saying nothing.

'This afternoon, now, I might have run, but not any longer. They can't manhandle me like they did and get away with it.'

Buck nodded, still silent. He wanted to remain impartial on this point. Of course, he wanted the Shermans to stay, but he would leave that decision up to them. Then, if the worst did happen, they could not blame him any more than they did at the present moment.

He knew that Jack Lacey's wife, Frances Lacey, had made a couple of public statements, down in town, that she blamed nobody but one Buckley Wilson for getting her husband into this serious trouble.

Laura Fromberg had told him about Mrs. Lacey's statement. This had hurt him more than he cared to admit. For before each settler had picked out his homestead, Buck had made it plain to him the situation here on Burnt Wagon range.

Later, after much questioning, he had received similar assurances from Martha Buckman that Mrs. Lacey had made this statement a number of times, once or twice in her store.

'But don't think anything of it, Buck. Her tongue runs from both ends and the middle. Right after she got done saying it she had forgotten what she had said.'

'She meant it,' Buck had said.

He had braced Jack Lacey on the subject. Jack had cursed and said he'd talk to his woman—no woman was going to run him. Buck had asked him not to mention it to Frances.

'Heck, I'm not runnin',' Jack Lacey had maintained.

Now Spike Sherman was talking again, talking in a low voice. 'I was raised in the slums. Lots of times us kids didn't have enough to eat. We used to steal food, and we stole it to live.'

Buck heard a movement behind him, and a quick glance told him Shannon Sherman stood in the doorway. Her husband evidently had not heard her arrival. Doc Crow sat on the chair, thick legs parted, hands dangling down over his bag, sitting on the floor between his feet.

'I could get my old job back at that stinkin' leather factory, maybe. Twelve hours a day in a stinkin' room with the vats. I could come home, weary and tired, and we'd live in the slums.'

Buck glanced at Shannon. Her face was pale in the lamplight, her lips were wet. She watched her husband.

'Not for me. I've got my land, and while this house isn't no mansion, it's the best we've ever had. When I get done with it, I'll have runnin' water from the spring. No, I'm not goin' run, Buck.'

Buck said, 'I'll be with you, boy.'

Spike Sherman still stared up at the ceiling.

'That's all we need, Buck. You an' me an' Lacey and Smith. Yep, an' Tim McCarty, bless his Irish soul, an' good ol' Horace Browning. Yes, an' now this fur buyer, he's with us, too, ain't he?'

'He's part of the bunch.'

'We'll stay united. And by heck, we'll whip them, if we stick together.' He looked at Buck, and then he saw his wife standing there, holding the lamp and listening.

'What do you say, Shannon?'

Shannon looked at Buck, her lips trembling. She looked at Doc Crow, who stared at the floor. Then she looked at her young husband.

By now, Buck saw, her fright had changed to a deep, strong strength. It seemed that this trouble had hardened her, had drawn her through fire, and thereby had made her strong and calm.

'Your words are my words, Spike.'

Doc Crow said, 'Now you get to sleep, young man. Your jaw sure isn't broken, not with the spiel you been giving. How's my baby?'

'She's in her crib,' Shannon Sherman said.

Doc said, 'Got to see my girl before I go.'

Doc Crow went into the little girl's room. Buck walked over to Spike and took his hand.

'I'll be out tomorrow with your team. Shannon left it in town and came out with us in Doc's rig. Anything you need from town?'

Spike looked at Shannon.

Shannon said, 'I might ride in with the Laceys when they drive by. They go in every

65

Saturday for groceries. That is, if Spike is well enough to let me go.'

'Tomorrow,' said Spike, 'I'll be patchin' fence.'

Buck and Doc Crow said little on the ride back to town. By this time the rain had stopped entirely and the sky was clear, with a rim of the moon showing over the hills.

'Tomorrow should be a nice day, Buck.'

'Hope so,' Buck said. 'I've still got sixty acres of seed to drill in.'

When they got to town Buck offered to put Doc's team away. Doc climbed down from the buggy, muttering something about a man getting old and stiff.

'I'd sure appreciate that, Buck.'

Buck unharnessed the team, grained the horses and saw they had fresh hay, then sought his own bed for a few hours' sleep.

CHAPTER SIX

The morning dawned bright and clear without a cloud in the sky. Buck was up early, and early forenoon found him riding toward his farm on Diamond Willow Creek.

His bronc pulled at the curb-bit, fresh from his long stay in the barn and filled with its oats and hay. A curlew ran ahead of them, chirping and making his wild call, seemingly glad that once again spring walked untroubled across this high northern rangeland.

He left the main road, and followed the road that led to his farm. The road continued past his gate, a brown set of lines running toward the Jack Lacey farm, which bordered Buck's homestead.

Buck opened the barbed-wire gate without dismounting, also shutting it while still in saddle. For a moment, then, he sat a silent kak, looking at the foothills that tumbled and ran to the north, finally meeting the Little Rockies, the blue mountains that seemed no more than stenciled lines against the northern horizon. The scene was one of desolation, and yet there was beauty in it. The beauty of clean, rain-washed distances, luring and beckoning with silent fingers.

Then the thought of the Rafter Y moved in, burying under its weight the sentimentality the sight of the blue Little Rockies had raised.

Hatchet Joe was milking the cow, and he looked up from his milk stool as Buck entered the barn.

'Nicee morning, Missee Buck.'

Buck asked, 'Everything all right?'

'Every little thing, she all light, Buck. Hatchet Joe, him sleep close to his lifle each an' evely night.'

Buck squatted, holding the reins of his horse. 'I suppose you heard about Darr Gardner jumping Glen Hatfield, eh?'

The Chinese nodded, milking rapidly. Milk jetted into the bucket and made a thick foam on the pail.

'Jack Lacey, him tell me when he go home last night. Missee Hatfield, him sick, huh?'

'He don't feel too well,' Buck said. 'I suppose you heard about Spike Sherman's trouble, too?'

The Oriental had not heard about Sherman being beaten by the Rafter Y men. Buck told him the story and watched the Chinese eyes squint a little at the corners. Hatchet Joe had known him ever since Buck's birth. He never seemed surprised or happy to any great extent.

'Tlouble, she bleak open at seams, like Ol' Man usta say, years ago.'

Buck told about the farmers' meeting to be held that night at their house. Hatchet Joe, his milking completed, stood up, kicking back his stool.

'Me, I get house leady. Makee plenty hot coffee.'

Buck carried one pail to the house. The Chinese strained the milk through a cheesecloth into flat milk pans, then set them

68

in the icebox to cool.

'You havee bleakfast, Buck?'

Buck said he had eaten in town, but he could stand some hot coffee. Hatchet Joe poured it, his monkey-like face puckered and serious.

There was nothing Buck could do at his farm. With the ground soaking wet, he could not seed wheat. He went into a plowed field and dug down to see how far in the moisture had sunk. The ground was wet down for over a foot. This kind of moisture would see crops up and tide them over until another rain came.

Hatchet Joe was mending harnesses.

Buck squatted beside the Chinese. 'I'm headin' back into town, Hatchet. I'm goin' to wire over to Chinook and ask the sheriff to come over or to send over a deputy.'

'If he send deputy, he no do nothin'.'

Buck straightened. 'Worth the try, though.'

He circled the Jack Lacey place, noticing that Lacey's wheat was breaking through the damp earth; he would have a good stand. This rain had come at the right time, no two ways about that.

He did not stop in at the Lacey farm. He was afraid Frances Lacey might pounce on him. She was an erratic woman, he figured—he'd had enough trouble the last twenty-four hours without tangling with an irate

69

housewife.

She was out lifting a bucket of water from the well when he rode by on the lope. He lifted his hand but did not stop. She waved back. Then the hill rose and hid the farmhouse from his sight.

All the creeks were full, roaring down to the river. By nightfall, if no more rain fell, the runoff would be gone and the streams would be again close to their normal size. Lots of good water—water that could be used for irrigation—was going to waste.

That was another angle he intended to develop, if and when the Rafter Y gave him and his farmers time to develop an irrigation system. He had talked about it with the county surveyor over in Chinook. At that time the man had not seemed very interested. No doubt, Buck knew, because of fear of Darr Gardner.

Gardner controlled quite a few votes, and the surveyor had a soft job he aimed to hang onto—he did not want to incur the disfavor of a man as politically powerful as Gardner.

But a man could dam up any of these creeks, run irrigation ditches out below the dam, and put water across his fields. Very few of these creeks went dry, even in the most hot and arid summer.

But that was still in the future.

He talked with Horace Browning, who was out building fence. The husky Porcupine Creek farmer sank his fence bar with great force as Buck told him about Darr Gardner and Len Huff beating up young Spike Sherman.

'Darn it, Buck, we can't let them get away with this.' Buck nodded. 'We'll talk it over tonight when we meet at my farm. I kinda hate to leave our farms deserted, though. You'll have nobody at your place; neither will the other bachelors and single men. An' that includes Jones and Smith and McCarty, too.'

'Have to chance it,' Browning said. 'Them Rafter Y men won't know about us meetin' nohow, will they?'

'Not unless one of us farmers tells them,' Buck said.

'We kin leave our lamps lit, like we was home, Buck. That'd fool 'em, I figure. This is a big kentry, though, an' a man could hit almost any place he wanted, at any time he wanted.'

Buck agreed with that.

'Well, gotta git along with this fence. Come the first wheat I sell, I'm sendin' back East for the woman an' the boy. Henry jes' turned seventeen the other day. He's our only boy.'

Buck sensed the loneliness and homesickness in the thick man's words. He got the impression some of his farmers were really fighting two battles: the first was to develop and cultivate their new farms in opposition to the Rafter Y; the second was to fight the loneliness that was in them for their families and relatives back East.

'We should have good crops, if we get another rain around the Fourth of July,' Buck said.

'That's right.'

Buck Wilson headed back for town, putting his horse at a long trot. He braced his hands against the fork of his saddle, whistling a little. The sun was warm, the rain had come at the right time, and in a few days the soil would be dry enough so he could go back to seeding his wheat.

Once he saw two riders, angling across the rim of the southern hills, and his glasses showed them to be a couple of Rafter Y boys he knew. Evidently they were out hunting Rafter Y strays, keeping them away from the lower flats, where the runoff from the creeks had made bog holes.

He retied his glasses onto his saddle.

He stopped in at the Sherman ranch, intending to see how Spike had spent the night, but nobody was at the place except the Sherman collie. The dog came out barking, fangs clicking. Buck reined his horse back, speaking softly to the dog. But the dog did not fall for soft words.

Buck was glad he was not on the ground. That collie, he figured, would tackle a man on foot. He was a good watchdog.

'Hello, the house.'

No answer, only the echo of his voice among the wet cottonwood trees back of the ranch house.

'Call off your dog.'

Still no answer.

Buck reined his horse back, the collie snapping at his forefeet. Evidently the Sherman family had gone to town with the Laceys or some other farmer who had gone into Burnt Wagon for his Saturday shopping.

He whirled his bronc and hit him with his spurs. The dog closed in, but the horse kicked up mud and gravel from its shod hoofs. This hit the dog in the face, stopping him.

Buck glanced down. The collie stood beside the gate, barking at him. Buck Wilson put his horse down the lane, heading for town.

With the entire Sherman family gone from their farm, that meant that Spike had been well enough to go into town. Then another thought hit Buck. Maybe Spike had got worse and they had taken him into the doctor.

He doubted that. Still, a man never knew. Before leaving town he had talked with Doc

Crow. Doc had said that Glen Hatfield was still very sick.

A rider came off the hills and he recognized Laura Fromberg. A frown rose, furrowing his forehead. What was she doing out here on the range? True, she was a great one to go out horseback riding alone, he knew.

Once he had met her way over by the Rafter Y spread.

'Hello, Buck.'

He pulled his horse to a walk. 'Hello, Laura. Where you been?'

'Rock gathering.'

Buck waved his hand. 'Well, there's no shortage of them, Laura. Going to use them in class work?'

'We're studying just a little bit of geology, Buck.'

Buck smiled. He liked the looks of her, sitting her black gelding. She sure knew how to ride, he thought. She sat a horse almost as well as Martha Buckman. Now that was odd, wasn't it? Every time he met Laura Fromberg, he found himself comparing her with Martha.

'Hope you know more about geology than I do,' Buck said.

She said she had taken a semester of geology in teacher's college. Buck did not ask her where she had gone to school. He was not one to go prying into another person's past. And the word *school* still brought a shiver to him.

He never had been much of a scholar. School had been a punishment thought up by people who wanted to keep kids miserable in a room when they wanted to be out in the saddle or down swimming in the creek.

They chatted about other things, with Laura talking most of the time. Buck was content to listen. She was sorry he wasn't going to the dance. Darr Gardner had asked her to go with him, but she did not care to attend the dance with the Rafter Y owner.

Buck found himself wondering just what had turned her against the Rafter Y man. But he did not ask any questions. If she wanted to tell him, that was her business. If she did not care to, that was still all right.

Then a thought came from out of nowhere, stung him like a bee, and buzzed back into the mystic nowhere whence it had come.

Maybe she would not go with Darr Gardner, because she wanted to go with him.

He examined that, wondering whether he should be flattered or alarmed. He decided it had both elements. He was complimented because he was male and a healthy male—apparently a woman sought his company more than that of any other man. It alarmed him, too, just a little, but he couldn't lay his finger

75

on the exact cause of that alarm. Once he had heard that when a woman set out to trap a man, she always came back with his hide.

Well, whoever got him would get a man who sure was broke in the pocketbook, he thought, smiling.

'What's so amusing, Buck?'

He came back to his saddle with a visible start. 'I was jest thinkin' somethin', Laura.'

He saw her pretty frown. She was dark and lovely, and this affected him. She was slightly worried, too. He knew why. His words had shut her off from his thoughts, and she did not like that.

That seemed to be a fault with most women, he found himself thinking. When they got a man by marriage, they seemed to think the license was a certificate of ownership, even to a man's thoughts.

Then he thought: But I never feel that way around Martha.

'Thinking what, Buck?'

'Just how this rain helped us at the right time,' he fibbed.

'I don't see anything funny in that.'

He decided to change the subject. 'I suppose you heard about Spike Sherman being beat up?'

'I have. But when I rode out this way I met the Shermans going into town with the

Laceys. Mr. Sherman was sitting in the back, holding the baby.'

'Glad to hear he's better,' Buck said.

The rest of the ride into Burnt Wagon was silent for the most part. Buck got the impression she was pouting a little because she had not learned the nature of his mirth.

Well, he wasn't married to her, he wasn't.

They parted in front of the schoolhouse which was set on the west end of town.

'Good-bye, Buck.'

'Bye, Laura.'

CHAPTER SEVEN

On that Saturday morning Darrell Gardner was in the saddle early, heading for Buggy Creek, where his men had finished a retainer dam a few weeks before. On that side of the Rafter Y range water sometimes became scarce when summer's heat dragged on. Therefore he had built a check dam to hold water for his cattle who grazed on that end of his ranch.

With Buggy Creek dry, his cattle would have to walk about five miles for water, getting water from Diamond Willow Creek, which never went dry, even in the severest drought. Gardner had reasoned that a fat cow was one that had plenty of water and grass at hand. And a cow wouldn't put on beef by hiking to Diamond Willow Creek each day. The trip would incur ten miles of travel. And in those ten miles would be expended a lot of beef.

He was riding a big black, a fancy-looking, high-stepping horse. He rode out of the Rafter Y before any of his punchers or his foreman was awake. The hostler slept on his cot in the barn but the Rafter Y owner did not awaken him. He saddled his horse, led him out the back door without awakening the flunky, found his stirrup and loped toward Buggy Creek.

The few hours he had spent at his ranch had been without rest. He had paced the room, adding this against that, trying to gather some total which forever kept evading him. He had drawn first blood against the farmers.

He had whipped Glen Hatfield. Together he and Len Huff had downed young Spike Sherman. This would get around and all the farmers would hear of it. Some of them, he figured, would be afraid. Some might be so afraid they might pull stakes. He didn't know. He hoped so . . .

There was but one fly in the ointment. Buckley Wilson had knocked Len Huff back, and that was a mark against the Rafter Y man. A mark in favor of the farmers was one against him, Darr Gardner.

Well, they'd get Buck Wilson, he figured.

Accordingly he shoved the thought of Buck back into an unused corner of his mind. He gave full thought to the legality of this fight. He knew it held no legality. The farmers were on land they had, by using their homestead-rights, acquired through legal tactics. The only way he could make them move was by using illegal tactics. And would this get by?

He figured the railroad officials might holler a little. They wanted farmers in for their own greedy purpose. A railroad was built to carry products—cattle, grain, wool, or the like. If farmers were moved in, then it was logical the railroad would have more products to ship to Eastern markets. With full freight trains, the railroad would, of course, profit.

Then, too, the railroad made money on each farmer by shipping him West. He took along his farming equipment and household goods; these demanded freight charges. Yes, the railroad officials might protest.

Whom could they appeal to?

The local law, of course. The sheriff, over in Chinook. And this thought brought a wide smile to Darr Gardner. The sheriff was an old friend of his. They'd punched cows together, drunk coffee out of the same tin can together. No. He didn't have to worry too much about the sheriff, he mused.

The sheriff was an old gent and he wanted his soft job. And he, Darr Gardner, had delivered plenty of votes from this section, and he could still command quite a block of votes.

He had it all figured out. The railroad company would get in touch with the sheriff, and the sheriff would obligingly ride over to Burnt Wagon himself, or send over a deputy he could trust. Yes, he could trust the deputy to do exactly nothing, and turn in a report that Burnt Wagon Basin was as peaceful as a lamb grazing beside his mother in an alfalfa field.

But what if the farmers appealed to Uncle Sam?

This problem troubled him. He had no influence with any federal men in Great Falls and, had he any friends, it would have undoubtedly done him no good, had this protest reached the ears of the government authorities. Yet he doubted if much could be done in a short length of time, and he did not intend these farmers to be here come autumn.

He knew the government, once getting to action, moved very slowly, bound up by jealousy and red tape between departments. By the time homestead authorities did get to

80

Burnt Wagon Basin for an investigation, there would be no farmers left to investigate, if his plans worked out.

These points covered, he gave himself to a study of the range. The rain had done him much good, also. Grass would grow long and green, and down on the flats the wind would roll it end over end, a green sea moving and bending under the wind. Good grass meant fat cattle. Fat cattle meant good markets.

He found Buggy Creek and rode along it. Even below the dam there was quite a flow of water. This, he knew, came over the spillway. Rafter Y cattle were back in the foothills where the soil was drier, and a number of times he detoured into the hills to look at his stock.

He had good cattle. Good-blooded cattle.

Most of the Montana cowmen ran Texas cattle. They were scrawny, hard-keeping beasts, long of neck and long of horn. They ranged far and ate more than a good-blooded steer, and never gained the weight that a good steer gained, even if they did graze down more grass.

He had bought good Hereford bulls in Iowa, shipped them out, and his herd had shown the effects of good breeding. He had some three-year-olds he aimed to ship come fall that sure would tip the scales. Three of them would weigh as much as five longhorns. And three cows never ate nearly the grass that five did.

He had pride in his ranch.

He found one cow in the bog. Her calf had gone asleep on an island and the high water had surrounded him. The cow had tried to get over to him and she had been bogged.

She was down to her belly in mud, but the water had receded away from her. The calf stood on the island in Buggy Creek and bawled. The island was entirely surrounded with water, but not very deep, he figured. He decided to get the cow out after he had dragged the calf off his water-surrounded strip of land.

He splashed across the water, his big black pawing the muddy water, and the calf, seeing him coming, bolted, tail up. The young bull hit the water, swam a little, then his hoofs found ground. He kicked up water and ran toward the foothills, tail up.

The cow bawled, struggling against the bog, but she could not get out. Big Darr Gardner studied her, all the time uncoiling his lasso. He built a big loop in the rope. Then, getting his black as close as he could without bogging him, he whirled the immense loop, got his momentum on stirrups, and made his cast.

He had intended that the rope settle all around the cow. But it got hooked on her horns. He pulled it in, rebuilt the loop, and made his second cast. This time, the big loop encircled the whole cow.

The cow bawled and the calf stopped and bawled back.

He took his dallies around his saddle-horn, wondering idly how many hundreds of cows he had jerked out of bogs. His dallies taken to his satisfaction, he turned the black so his rump was toward the cow; the horse moved against the rope.

Gardner's saddle settled under the pull. The black's hindquarters sank down, pulled down under his pull on the rope. The rope grew taut, tightening around the cow, pulling shut like a draw string on a sack.

Gardner said, 'Pull, Blacky, pull,' and touched the horse with his spurs, the black lurched a little, and he knew he had the cow loose then. Suddenly the animal was pulling the cow ahead, the cow struggling to get up. But she could not get to her feet, for the rope had pulled her four feet together.

Gardner looked back, smiling at her efforts. He pulled her on her side for about ten feet, then turned his black around. This allowed slack to come into the catch rope.

The cow kicked, got her hoofs free, and

stood up. She was wet and cold and muddy and she was mad. She stomped the ground, pawed up dirt, and swung her horns menacingly. But Darr Gardner did not let her attack his black.

He doubled the catch rope, making a whip out of it, and he came in from behind the critter, the rope working like a quirt. The cow gave up and loped toward her waiting calf, all her fight gone.

Gardner watched her, coiling his rope. 'Good bossy,' he said.

He rode up Buggy Creek, strapping his lasso again to the fork of his hull. He found no more cows in bogs, and at last he came to the check dam his men had built in the creek.

The dam was holding well. They had faced it with gravel and rock, and over this had pounded in concrete. Water was tossing through the spillway, muddy and foamy, but it did not eat into the rock and concrete spillway.

Gardner folded his hands across his saddle-horn, content and watching his creation. It was like the immense Rafter Y. It was sturdy. Just as the Rafter Y defied the onslaughts of the farmer, so did this Rafter Y check dam defy these flood waters.

It would stand, just as the Rafter Y would stand.

He looked beyond the dam toward the northern hills, now green with buckbrush and grama grass. His gaze went over these hills, measuring them and finding them good, and his eyes rested on the blue cones of the Little Rockies, wavering and dim against the sky.

He was at the far end of his range—the most desolate section on which he ran cattle. Therefore he was surprised when he heard a horse clash a hoof on rock, the sound coming from behind him.

He turned on stirrups, hand going under his slicker to anchor itself on his holstered gun. But he did not draw the gun. He recognized the rider and slowly his hand came back, and all the while a frown formed on his wide forehead.

'You shouldn't ride behind a man like that.'

The rider was astraddle a black, too.

'I saw you from the hills. You're jumpy, Darr.'

'You should be more careful. This is range war. You should call to a man before you ride behind him.'

'Next time,' the rider said.

Darr Gardner looked at the rider. Gardner looked at the rider's black gelding. He said, 'You've ridden a long ways. What is it?'

'You're abrupt.'

'People don't ride this far just to pass the

85

time of day. You have something you want to tell me. What is it?'

The rider was silent, looking across space. Gardner thought: There's something over there, and looked at the hills, too. Then he realized the rider was only playing a waiting game, and he felt the raw pull of anger.

'What is it?'

'I have some information you might want to know. Tonight the farmers are going to meet in a body at Buck Wilson's house.'

'Who told you?'

'Wilson himself.'

Gardner lifted his right hand and stroked his jaw. He had not shaved that morning because of the rawness of his face and he did not like the feel of his whiskers. He liked to be clean and smoothshaven.

He could not see good out of one eye, but the swelling was leaving it and the pain had left long ago.

'Thanks.'

'What's it worth?'

Gardner said, 'You're to the point.'

'I need money. I always need money.'

Gardner said, 'Here's twenty bucks.'

The rider looked at the gold piece, and then it disappeared.

Gardner said, 'I'll ride a ways with you.'

'No.'

86

'Why not?'

'Somebody might see us. We can't afford that.'

'I'll see you tonight?'

But before the rider could answer, the black was loping back toward the hills. Darr Gardner watched the horse and rider reach the hills and then he lost sight of them as they rode up a wide coulee.

He sat there, thinking.

So they would meet at Buckley Wilson's house. That was good news. For while they were at the meeting, some of the farms would be unguarded. He ran over their locations in his mind.

Smith, over on Cottonwood Creek; McCarty, on Summit Creek; Lacey—who lived next to Buck Wilson—no, not Lacey. His wife would be at home, and so would Shannon Sherman. Jake Jones, over on Squaw Butte Flats. Yes, and Horace Browning, alone on Porcupine Creek.

Browning, he was the one. His farm was the farthest from Buck Wilson's, and therefore it would take longer to ride there from Buck's place. And there was no use in being caught at the job.

No use in courting danger.

Well, he'd ask Len Huff, and they would talk it over.

He rode the rest of Buggy Creek to the point where it formed, back in the rough country. And, all the time, his mind kept swinging back to the knowledge the rider had imparted.

He ate dinner in a line camp. These line camps all had chuck in them, for they had saved many a cowpuncher's life in the wintertime, when a blizzard had caught him far from the home ranch—too far to buck his way in facing a howling norther.

He opened a can of beans, made coffee, and then lay on the bunk, looking at a magazine. But the magazine refused to claim his interest. He threw it aside, clamped his hands behind his head, and looked up at the rafters in the ceiling, seeing them and yet not seeing them.

He went over this, feeling its corners, judging its position. And again decided they would hit Horace Browning's outfit. That decision made, he let it rest. Finally, he slept.

At two he was in saddle again, heading for the home ranch. He was north of the ranch, riding down Beaver Creek. Luck was with him, for he found no bogged cattle. One cow, though, had died in a flash flood, and he found her bloated, swollen carcass washed against a dam made of debris the water had swept down from the hills.

'Coyote bait,' he told his black.

He came into the ranch at about four-thirty. This was the slack season, yet he kept a full crew; his men were pitching horseshoes, for they always had Saturday afternoon off. He sat saddle and judged them and did not like what he saw.

They were cowhands, that was all. Would they fight for the spread that paid their wages, if that spread got in a tight?

Maybe . . . maybe not.

Then he remembered that he had not paid allegiance to any of the Texas outfits that had hired him for a few bucks a month, ropes and beans. When a man acquired property, then he also acquired greed, it seemed.

He also figured the other fellow should fight with him just because he was drawing wages from him.

Human nature, he guessed.

One cowboy said, 'Well, dog-gone it, Smoky got a ringer. Now watch me pile another right on top of his to make it no good!'

'No can do, Shorty!'

'You jes' watch, wiseacre.'

The horseshoe sailed out, flipped once, then clanged around the peg. Smoky spat and threw his hat to the ground.

'Lucky stiff.'

'Not luck,' Shorty said modestly. 'Science.'

The hostler came and took Darr Gardner's

black.

'Oats him good, an' give him fresh hay after you water him. Where is Len Huff?'

The old man jerked a thumb toward the foreman's cabin.

'In his bunk, I reckon.'

Gardner unbuckled his chaps and hung them on a peg driven into a log on the barn. He took loose his spurs and hung them over the peg, too.

When he came into Huff's cabin his nostrils took in the smell of gear and fresh tobacco smoke. Huff lay on his bunk, pipe in hand, newspaper in the other.

'Howdy, boss.'

Gardner nodded and sat down. Huff, watching him, was silent. Finally Darr Gardner spoke.

'The farmers are meetin' tonight at Buck Wilson's house.'

Huff nodded, his sunken eyes wise.

CHAPTER EIGHT

The depot operator had said, 'That'll be a buck an' eight cents,' and Buck had dug down and paid him.

'Tell the operator at Chinook I want a

return reply,' Buck said.

The man studied the telegram blank that Buck had filled. He was a railroad man and he had no ties in this trouble and therefore he was neutral. His lips formed the words aloud.

'That right, Buck?'

'That's it,' Buck returned.

Without further word, the man had sat down and tapped out his message on his key, the sound making a metallic loudness in the depot. Buck and the operator were alone in the building.

The key stopped clattering.

'How long until a return comes?' Buck asked.

'All depends on the sheriff,' the operator said. 'This will have to go to Williston, then go back to the Great Northern. The message will be in Chinook in about half an hour.'

'Beats ridin' that distance,' Buck grunted. 'Well, I'll mosey over town, an' then report back later.'

'No percentage in stickin' around here, unless you craves my company.'

Buck grinned and winked. 'I could do almighty well without that, Charlie.'

He went to the hotel and saw Glen Hatfield. The man claimed he'd be up on his feet soon but Buck thought otherwise, judging from what Doc Crow told him and the appearance

91

of the hide buyer. For Glen Hatfield's face was pale, his whiskers standing out like black wires on the waxen skin.

The old proprietor was in the lobby when the land locator went back toward the street, and he gave Buck a long, dour look as he peered over his gold-rimmed spectacles. Buck gave him a short nod.

'When's thet feller leavin' thet bed, Wilson?'

'Why the sudden rush?'

'Me, I don't cotton to my hotel becomin' a hosterpistol, I don't.'

Buck said, 'Hatfield will leave that bed when Doc Crow says he is able to leave. Until then he stays in bed whether or not that bunk is in your lousy hotel. An' when I say *lousy*, I mean just that!'

The old man glared at him, the tips of his mustaches jumping as if somebody had a match under them and they were jerking away from the heat.

'Two things I never did cotton to, fella. One is sheepherders an' the other is a hoeman.'

Buck said, 'I've always disliked hotel owners.'

But there was no percentage in standing there and wasting breath on this narrow-minded old cowman who sold his cattle for a so-called hotel. Buck went outside, glad to be out in fresh air again.

He had some time to kill before his message would be answered, if the Chinook sheriff took the courtesy even to answer it. He decided that one pleasant place to kill that time in would be Buckman's Store.

Only one customer, Mrs. Wiggins, was in the store, and Buck sneaked a few crackers out of the barrel and munched on them. Martha glanced at him, then gave her attention to her customer.

'Yes, those colors will not run, Mrs. Wiggins. Why, Jennie Martin made a dress out of this material—same pattern, too—and she's washed it and washed it and it is still bright.'

Buck thought, as all males think in similar predicaments, *hogwash*. He chewed on a cracker and gave his thoughts over to the matter of the Chinook sheriff.

'Well, I'll get enough for a dress.'

Then followed some measuring, with Mrs. Wiggins as the model, and then some arithmetic, and finally the bargain was completed with Mrs. Wiggins, bundle under arm, going by Buck Wilson without even so much as a nod.

Buck shrugged. 'She doesn't like me, I guess.'

'She's for the cowmen,' Martha said. 'How

93

many crackers did you eat?'

'What difference does it make?'

'I'm not running a free cracker stand. If you want a free meal go down to the saloon and order a beer and get in on the free lunch.'

'You serious?'

'Certainly I'm serious.'

Buck saw then she was close to laughter.

'You danged women. No man'll ever understand you, I reckon. I'm killing time until I get ready to move on down the street.'

'Wish all I had to do was loaf.'

'Thanks,' he said wryly.

They bantered back and forth with words, each enjoying it. Finally Martha said, 'I heard you rode into town this morning with Laura Fromberg. I suppose that was an accident, or something. You sure you didn't take her out to look at your farm?'

'But . . .' Buck stopped. 'This town sure is full of eyes. I met her in the hills; she was out lookin' for rocks.'

'*For rocks!*' Martha laughed with a silvery note. 'I guess I've heard everything now. Well, here comes a victim.'

'Terrible way to speak of your customers.'

'They are victims, not customers, the minute they step in here,' she said airily. 'Now what is it today, Mrs. O'Higgins?'

Mrs. O'Higgins nodded at Buck, but the

nod seemed to cost her effort. Buck went out on the sidewalk again, thinking no man was ever a fit opponent for any woman. It seemed to him that women always hit below the belt.

And it seemed also that all the Burnt Wagon townswomen were partial to the Rafter Y. Well, that was only logical. Until his farmers had come the big Rafter Y payroll had supported the town.

But Martha had told him, on the quiet, that her trade had doubled since the farmers had moved in. She knew that the more people there were in the community, the better business would be.

But try to tell that to any other businessman, Buck reflected.

A boy came along, rolling a hoop. 'My ol' man's got a telegram for you, Wilson. He tol' me to tell you.'

'Thanks, Jimmy.'

Jimmy wrinkled his freckled nose. 'Sure figured it would be worth a dime to you, anyway.'

'Not such a small thing as a dime, Jimmy.'

'How much more then?' The kid was hopeful.

'It isn't worth anything,' Buck said.

The kid muttered something, then spat in disgust. He hitched up his pants and went down the street, rolling his hoop and hollering, 'Chug, chug, I'm a train. Get out of my way, Carl!'

The operator had written out the message, and he slid the paper to Buck with: 'Fast work, eh?'

Buck nodded and read. The sheriff was sending over his under-sheriff, James McClellan, who would be in Burnt Wagon in three days, maybe four. He would dispatch Mr. McClellan tomorrow morning.

'Hope he's better than General McClellan,' Buck said, grinning.

He stuck the message in his pocket. His farmers would like to read it.

'That's collect at this end,' the operator said.

Buck said, 'The dirty dog,' and paid.

He had no reason for staying in town, so he ate at the Broken Spur, where Wong Ling plied him with questions and curses, all directed toward the Rafter Y and anybody who was against his countryman, Hatchet Joe. Buck got the impression that Hatchet Joe could commit mass murder by the use of quicklime and it would be all right with Wong Ling.

When he rode past the schoolhouse, Laura came out and called to him.

'I want you to look at my rock display.'

'Well . . .' he answered with uncertainty.

'You have lots of time. Get off your horse.'

He looked back toward Burnt Wagon. 'Some ol' maid of either sex is right now spyin' on us, Laura. They even talked when we rode into town this morning. I don't want to ruin your reputation. Me, I ain't got one.'

'Oh, fiddlesticks.'

Buck dismounted and walked into the schoolroom, spurs jangling. She had six grades in one room and therefore the seats were arranged according to size. The rocks were in a glass case a pupil had made.

'They look all right to me,' Buck said. 'They look like they're made of hard material.'

'What a joke!'

He looked down at her, grinning. He didn't know how it happened, but she was suddenly in his arms. Her head was up, her eyes closed, her lips opened slightly. His head came down. Her arm came around his neck and he felt the ardor of her lips. When he broke away, his brain was on a merry-go-round.

'My gosh, what happened to bring on that?'

'I liked it, Buck.'

Buck thought: You sure did. He knew he shouldn't stay but a moment. He was sure somebody was watching from town, waiting to see how long he stayed in the building.

'Come on to the dance, Buck, please.'

'Well, I'll come in after the meetin', but I might not get in until around midnight.'

'Try to come.'

When he got on his bronc, he was a little flustered. She had put her arm around his neck and pulled his head down. Still, it didn't seem too genuine. For some reason, there seemed a lot of play-acting in it.

She seemed too ardent, just a little too enthusiastic.

When he was out of sight of the schoolhouse he ran his fingers to his lips. He had kissed two girls in two days. Well, if he didn't watch out, he would be in a mess of trouble. A man couldn't marry two women.

He touched spurs to his horse, and found himself wishing he had not kissed Laura. And why?

Well, she was a nice young woman, educated and smart, and she was pretty, too. Most men would be tickled blue to claim her as a bride. Still, she had always seemed a little too hard, a little too calculating, he thought.

He had got this impression the first time he saw her. He had been down at the depot, waiting for some express to come in—a new plowshare he had ordered from Great Falls— and she had stepped down the steps, walking behind the fat salesman from that wholesale house. When he first saw her he thought: She looks city-like, all right. Those people who live in cities seem to lose all pity for their fellowmen. To me, her face looks sort of hard-like.

Then she had looked at him, and he had thought there was a hardness in her eyes, too. Even before he had been formally introduced to her, he had received that impression of craftiness and stealth.

When he had finally got to know her, that feeling had left him somewhat. Yet now, for some reason, it was strong in the saddle with him.

He put his bronc to a lope, heading for his Diamond Willow ranch.

CHAPTER NINE

They came on horseback and in buggies. Dick Smith and Tim McCarty drove over in the Irishman's lumber wagon. They tied their horses and teams among the cottonwoods along Diamond Willow Creek and came into Buck's house.

They were a pretty grim bunch. Even Tim McCarty, who was usually joking in his wide Irish brogue, was not so gay and free with his wisecracks. The Irishman's blue eyes were stormy.

Horace Browning was the last to arrive. He came in on his blue roan plowmare, riding an old army saddle he had picked up back East in a junk shop. He tied his mare and clomped his work brogues toward the house.

'Always late, Horace,' joked Jack Lacey.

'Me, I'm a slow man, gents.'

'You live too far from nowhere,' Sherman said.

Somebody asked, 'How's the jaw, Spike?'

Buck saw the deadly hate that suddenly colored the young man's eyes. But when Spike Sherman spoke his voice sounded as usual.

'Gittin' along fine, Jake. I must have a jawbone like the one Samson used to beat up all them Bible fellas with, eh?'

They laughed at that, but the laughter did not run long, Buck noticed. Hatchet Joe came in with his big coffee pot and filled cups. Buck got a gallon of whiskey out of the cupboard and asked if anybody *didn't* want a shot. Browning was the only one who did not want a drink. Buck did not press him to take a shot of the whiskey.

Each man had his own scruples, his own principles, his own beliefs. And it was up to his neighbors to respect his integrity. If all people did that there would be no wars, Buck thought grimly.

Hatchet Joe had arranged their chairs in the living room, moving the table to the head of the room. The men sat there, sipping coffee, some spiking their coffee with whiskey. Buck waited until they were more or less in a freer mood, then called the meeting to order.

Briefly he outlined the preceding events: the fight between Hatfield and Gardner, omitting how he had knocked Huff back into the crowd. He told about Gardner and Huff jumping Spike Sherman. They knew all these things, of course; but they listened, and each seemed to be wondering how this would end.

Buck said, 'Mr. Hatfield is very sick. Doc Crow is sure the man has internal hemorrhages.'

'What if he dies?' Spike Sherman asked, speaking slowly because of his sore jaw.

'We will file a murder charge against Gardner,' Buck replied.

He told about wiring over to Chinook to the sheriff.

'The sheriff said he would send over James McClellan, his under-sheriff. He leaves Chinook tomorrow by horseback across country.'

'That won't do no good,' Horace Browning grunted.

'Anyway,' Buck said, 'we filed a legal process. Now, if we have to use guns to defend our property, we can use bullets with the assurance that at least we have sought protection from the law.'

'That ain't much assurance,' Jack Lacey put in. 'That sure wouldn't stop a bullet, Buck.'

'Wasn't intended for that,' Buck answered.

He brought up the subject of guns. Should they or should they not pack pistols? This brought on a rather lively discussion. One school of thought held that if they did pack weapons, then Gardner or Huff—or some Rafter Y puncher—might drive them into a gunfight.

If they did not pack guns, the worst that could come out of it would be a fist fight, for even if Gardner was a political power, this range would never stand for an armed man shooting down an unarmed man.

'Not even if the gent that don't pack a gun is just a farmer?' Tim McCarty smiled widely.

Browning was the one who was advocating a no-gun rule.

'That joke,' Browning said sternly, 'does not fit this predicament, Tim.'

McCarty's ruddy face went red in the lamplight.

'Some people,' McCarty said, seeming to speak to them all, 'seem to want to live forever. I'd rather kick the bucket fightin' for my rights, begorra, than run like a coward away from danger, I would.' And his jaw went out belligerently.

Buck glanced at Hatchet Joe, who stood behind the group. Hatchet Joe was grinning from ear to ear.

Buck said consolingly, 'You are both entitled to your opinions. This is an open meeting and nothing said here should create hard feelings. We're here for to arrive at a policy of action.'

'Then I say to hit at the Rafter Y,' Tim McCarty said harshly.

Browning said, 'That move would only result in unneeded warfare, and they have us outnumbered, too. They'd kill us off.'

Buck had to agree with Horace Browning. So did the rest of the farmers. He gave the floor to Jake Jones.

Jones rose to his small height, his face serious for once. He pointed out that when you chopped the head off a rattlesnake that snake then died. The head of this trouble was in the persons of Len Huff and Darr Gardner. In fact, it was a two-headed snake, but Gardner was the main head.

'What's your point?' Browning asked.

'I'll point it out for you.' Jake Jones grinned good-naturedly. 'We get rid of Gardner and Huff, and this trouble is over. The rest of the

Rafter Y hands are only hired hands, no more. They won't die for the Rafter Y. They haven't enough at stake.'

Browning was persistent. 'How will we get rid of Gardner and Huff?'

'There are two ways. Jail 'em or kill 'em off.'

Browning shook his head, pipe set between his teeth at a stubborn angle. Buck knew the man was very religious and wanted peace. But Browning did not seem to realize that to win peace sometimes a man has to use the implements of war. He decided this phase of the meeting was just turning into wasted words.

'Take a vote on that gun-totin' idea?' Dick Smith spoke.

Hatchet Joe gave each man a slip of paper and a pencil. Then, after they had written either yes or no, the Chinaman collected them and handed them to Buck. Buck called out the nature of each vote and Browning recorded them.

Buck did not vote. Being president of the grangers, his vote would be used only in event of a tie vote. And this vote was not a tie. Of the six farmers, five had voted *yes*. One voted *no*.

Buck knew that the *no* vote had come from Horace Browning.

'Then it is decided an' passed that hereafter we tote pistols on our persons, an' rifles out in the fields or on our saddles.'

'Not me.' Browning shook his head.

Buck did not press the matter. If the farmer did not want to carry a pistol, he did not need to.

Browning said, 'I do believe this trouble is being overrated, gentlemen. Just because Hatfield and Gardner fought is no sign we are in a range war. Maybe, unknown to us, Mr. Hatfield had some trouble with Gardner before the fist fight that we know nothin' about.'

'Maybe so, Horace.' Young Spike Sherman spoke slowly but his words held a touch of sarcasm. 'But what about them jumpin' on me? I'd never had no prior trouble with either of them.'

'I still think this is overrated,' Browning insisted.

Browning did not see the look and the shake of the head that Buck Wilson sent to young Sherman. There was no use in exchanging viewpoints with somebody who had his mind made up and was unwilling to change it.

Sherman shook his head, registering disgust.

Buck quickly introduced another subject. His plan was to let things ride until Under-

Sheriff James McClellan reported on Burnt Wagon range.

'The best thing, I figure, is to wait and see what his report will be,' the land locator said. 'For myself, I can see no reason for tying into the Rafter Y. Let's play a waiting game.'

'Unless they force us too much,' Spike Sherman added.

Buck nodded. 'Unless they force us, Spike.'

They took a vote on that. This time, all voted in the affirmative. Buck looked down at his notes and saw the agenda had been run through. They had all blown off steam, and all had profited thereby. Yes, and a plan of action had been created that all seven of them favored.

Jake Jones, short and wiry, sat deep in his chair, chin in his hand, watching Buck. Dick Smith had his bulk crammed into his chair, barely able to get between the arms. Beside Dick Smith sat Tim McCarty, red-faced, beefy, and pugnacious. Three good hands, Buck realized.

Of the three, Dick Smith was the most valuable, he reasoned. Smith was level-headed but so, for that matter, were the other two farmers. He swung his gaze over to Spike Sherman, who sat next to Tim.

Sherman was young, but he would do. He was smart and he wouldn't fly off the handle, even if the two Rafter Y men had beaten him. Buck looked to Jack Lacey, sitting next to Spike Sherman.

Lacey, he had to admit, was an unpredictable person.

Buck found himself wondering if Jack Lacey did not owe much of his uncertainty to his wife, for she nagged him a lot. Lacey had been a shoemaker back East, he knew. He had had a good business, but the indoor work had not been too healthy for him.

Well, time would tell.

He decided they were a pretty reliable bunch, brave enough for the most part, but inexperienced in this land and its inhabitants. They were from the East, and back there the land had been settled for generations, but this was a raw, new land, which, but a few short years ago, had been inhabited by redskins only.

All he could do was keep on working and hope for the best.

'More coffee?' Hatchet Joe asked.

'I'm so full of coffee now it's runnin' outta me ears,' Tim McCarty declared. 'I'll take another nip outta thet jug, an' then 'twill be on me way that this boy will be, gentlemen.'

Buck noticed that Tim's *nip* was about four hearty swallows. The Irishman was feeling the effects of his drinks.

Over the entire group had been an air of tension and unrest. Their homes, except in the cases of Lacey and Sherman, were being left unguarded. Yet nobody but themselves and Buck had known this meeting was going to be held. Therefore it was illogical that anybody would hit at their holdings, for the Rafter Y did not know about the gathering.

Buck closed the meeting.

They went for their rigs and saddles, talking as they went into the yard. Tim McCarty and Jack Lacey got into a heated discussion with Horace Browning about the Rafter Y.

Others listened, silent for the most part.

Hatchet Joe and Buck stood on the porch.

'Allee time, man he argue,' the Chinese said, spitting disgustedly.

Buck nodded, sleep on him. He had slept very little the night before. Then he remembered that Laura had wanted him to look in on the dance.

Would he ride into town? Six miles to town, and that seemed a long way, even with a fresh horse. Still, the dance ran until dawn, and he could whirl a few girls around.

He debated, listening with one ear to the discussion. And all the time he knew his mental debate was useless. He would ride in to the dance. Laura would be there, and Martha would also be there, after she closed her store.

He could sleep in his office instead of coming back to his farm. The soil was still so damp he couldn't seed wheat until Monday, if it would be dry enough then. This rain . . .

'Look, men!'

His harsh words broke up the endless argument. They turned and stared at him, the lamplight from the house lighting their upturned, tense faces.

'Over there! A fire!'

He had seen it first because he had stood on the porch and therefore was at a higher elevation. Now they turned as a unit, looking in the direction he pointed. For a moment there was a hushed silence.

Then somebody said, 'That's Horace's farm burning down!'

There could be no mistake. The only farm over that way belonged to Horace Browning. Already the flames were inching higher over the hills, yellow and distant and terrible against the night.

Browning said, 'Why I never left no fire in the stove. I saw sure it was out!' Then the real truth struck him and he looked up at Buck and Hatchet Joe, and Buck saw the terrible, naked anger in his usually peaceful eyes.

'They've torched my outfit, Buck.'

Buck was the general immediately. 'All you

109

men ride for your homes, except Browning. We all can't ride to the fire. For if we do, they might torch your homes while you were at Browning's.'

'Buck's right!'

'The dirty . . . Hit at a man when he ain't to home.'

Browning stared, not at the fire. His eyes were on Buck. He came up the steps, walking slowly, the lamplight on him.

'Buck,' he began, 'I was wrong. I'm going to strap on a gun an' . . .'

'Get for your farms!' Buck snapped. 'Ride fast, men! Stay at your farms the rest of the night!'

They ran for horses and rigs. Hoofs rang out and broncs left, scattering mud and gravel behind them that went spewing into the night. A buggy ran out, bumping over the soil, springs protesting. Hoofs beat into the night and ran out and became lost against the distance.

Tim McCarty cursed his team, and turning his wagon so sharply the front wheel cramped back and almost upset it. Dick Smith hung onto the seat, cursing the wild Irishman.

Buck said, 'Hatchet Joe, you stay here, savvy! Keep guard with a rifle, understand? I ride with Browning!'

'I keep guard! I swear over the graves of my

110

ancestors.'

Buck grinned, wondering what his ancestors would be thinking, if they knew. Browning was already in his old army saddle. He whipped the old blue roan mare around and loped to the barn, where Buck had led out his sorrel.

'Those dirty sons, Buck.'

Buck grunted, 'That's the way it'll be from here on,' and his saddle lifted. He kicked the sorrel in the belly, knocked the wind out of him, and tightened the cinch with a deft pull.

Hatchet Joe ran from the house, carrying a Winchester and a .45.

'Here, you takee this one, Buck. Ca'tlidges he in it an' here she is a box of bullets. You takee thees pistoloffer, Missee Blowning.'

Browning took the Colt and the box of shells.

CHAPTER TEN

Buck's sorrel took the lead, with the land locator bent against the wind, his spurs working. Behind him thundered the old work mare, her big hoofs plodding against the wet earth.

The sorrel was fast, a long-legged hill horse

that Buck had saved from the wreckage of his father's Bar S outfit. He could walk away from the old mare, wheezing and laboring behind him. But Buck did not let his cayuse leave Browning in the distance. He rode a stern rein, holding in the sorrel.

They headed toward the red flame that marked the position of Horace Browning's homestead cabin. Now a hill rose, cutting the flames from their view. Buck's sorrel scrambled upward, falling to his knees.

The land locator jerked the bronc upright. Their horses reached the summit, shod hoofs digging in the soft earth, their breathing labored. There on the summit they drew rein for a moment.

Buck noticed the flames were higher. Below them stretched Burnt Wagon Basin, dark and mysterious, with the jagged pin point of flame ahead, a needle against the night sky.

Browning said chokingly, 'It's gone, Buck, gone in flames! An' they've fired it! I know they have! I left not a bit of fire on the spread!'

'Sure burnin',' Buck had to admit.

There in the dim light the farmer turned a hawkish face toward Buck. 'Seems odd it would burn that fast when it just got through havin' a big rain on it. Seems mighty odd.'

'Kerosene on it, maybe?'

The hawkish face nodded dumbly. 'Yep,

an' them logs is green pine. Still got lots of pitch in them. Well, about the time we get there, Buck, the ashes will be a-gettin' cold, eh?'

Buck spoke almost too quietly for the farmer to hear.

'What was that, Buck?'

'Maybe we ain't ridin' over to your Porcupine Creek outfit, right now, Horace...'

Browning studied him. 'What do you mean by that, Buck?'

'One way to fight fire,' Buck reminded, 'is to fight it with another fire.'

Browning understood. 'You said a big mouthful, Buck. But where will we set this new fire?'

Buck clipped, 'At the Rafter Y spread itself.'

Browning nodded, watching his burning homestead buildings now. 'They got the tool shed an' the corrals an' that one barn set away from the other buildings a spell. Them buildin's I mentioned sure would make a good fire.' Browning wet a thumb and stabbed it into the night. 'Wind about right, too.'

'Good idea.'

Browning turned his old mare. 'But where will we get some kerosene, Buck? We want to get this thing off to a good start. While them

113

hellions is over burnin' down my outfit, we'll burn down part of theirs.'

'That Rafter Y line camp has a can of kerosene. They left it there to start a fire with an' to stoke the lamp. I mean that line camp down on Diamon' Willow Crick, Horace.'

'There'll be danger,' Browning said. 'They might have a guard out. An' it's my buildin's that got burned—not yours, Buck.'

'We're all in this together. Come on!'

He cake-walked his sorrel around, reins pulling. Then they were riding down the slippery, muddy hill, with the sorrel again in the lead. Behind him the old mare skidded and caught herself; then they hit the flat. Their broncs stretched out, and Browning used his quirt.

Buck rode with the corner of one eye on the horse and rider that thundered behind him. And he was forced to admit that the old mare had grit. She caught her second wind faster than did his sorrel and she drew up with him, with Browning a question mark over his old saddle.

'Wilson, I been a fool.'

Buck nodded, saying nothing.

'Me, I come from peaceful folks, people that looked down on violence. I thought back yonder this could be settled within the law.'

Buck hollered, 'We can't give up that idea

114

entirely, Horace.'

Browning went lower over his fork, his words shoved back by the wind. 'The law is the law we pack on our hips. Or in our middle holsters.'

He straightened then, this determination a part of him. Buck made no effort to break the man's sudden convictions.

Many thoughts pestered the land locator. He wished he knew who had ridden from the Rafter Y to the homestead of Horace Browning. Had Len Huff and Darr Gardner ridden over to set this fire?

That pair seemed the most logical choice of the entire Rafter Y crew. Buck knew every man on the Gardner spread with the exception of one or two new men who had been hired within the last month.

These new hands, he figured, were fancy with a gun, and were hired by Gardner for their gun speed. Maybe one or so of these new gunmen had set this fire?

Another thought kept darting across his mind. Maybe the Rafter Y had not torched the Browning homestead buildings? Maybe Browning *had* left a fire in the stove which had set fire to the buildings?

After all, they were not sure that the Rafter Y had really set the fire. This knowledge burned in Buck, seeking an answer. But then

115

logic, cold and sure and uncomforting, came in like a chilly blast, killing these conjectures.

Somehow Gardner had found out the farmers had all been at a meeting at his place. Then he had gone to the Porcupine Creek farm and torched it. And how did he know for sure?

To the south, over against the hills, was another fire.

Buck hollered, 'Look, Horace!'

Browning swung his old mare. He leaned forward on his stirrups, staring at the flame. Then he looked back at his own burning buildings.

'That other flame is Jack Lacey's barn. You know, not his big one; the shelter he made for his animals down in his cow pasture.'

Buck judged the probable location of the fire. Because of the night it was hard to determine on whose property this fire was exactly. Finally he conceded that the farmer was right.

He looked at Browning, who was watching him.

'That shows then that your fire was not an accident. Two fires don't occur at the same time accidentally. That means, too, that the Rafter Y has had two fire-settin' crews out.'

'That's right.'

Buck grunted something that sounded very

116

much like a curse.

'Well, Buck?'

'The same direction,' the land locator growled. 'We'll burn all of their buildings we can.'

'An' it'll take lead to stop us!'

Again they took up the mad, pounding pace. Buck's sorrel had his wind and pulled ahead again, but the old game mare kept close to the gelding's right flank. They threaded along the edge of Needle Gorge, the canyon below them.

Here they had to pull their broncs to a slower pace. One misstep and a bronc would be off that ledge, sliding down and down into space.

Buck hollered back, 'Be careful, Horace.'

But the old mare, weak in the knees, stumbled, and Buck hurriedly glanced back, fear tearing at his vitals. He saw Horace Browning sawing upward on the reins, and the man held the stumbling, frightened horse. Then the narrow trail was behind, and they were out on a wide mesa.

Browning panted, 'That was a close one.'

Buck nodded. He pointed toward some trees that made a darker line against the night.

'Yonder is the line camp.'

'Anybody there?'

'No light. Nobody there this time of the

117

year. They use it during the winter. Cowpunch stays there an' turns back drifting cattle.'

'Let's get that oil, Buck!'

Nevertheless, they circled the line camp once, just to make sure. Buck noticed that Horace Browning kept his gun in his fist, and this brought an amused smile to the land locator. The pacifism of the farmer had died before the cold-blooded arson of the Rafter Y.

They got down and went ahead. Buck stepped into the lean-to barn and reappeared with, 'No horse in here. Place is empty.'

They found the jug of kerosene in the corner where Buck had seen it when he had ridden this country the week before looking for one of his wandering milk cows. Now he shook it to verify its contents.

'Almost full.'

'We'll need lots of it.'

They were in saddle again, with Buck carrying the jug. And again they hit the trail, this time heading for the big Rafter Y to northeast. But the land locator did not set such a killing pace this time.

One question still bothered him. Who had told Darr Gardner that he and his farmers were meeting this night and therefore the homestead shack of Horace Browning would be without a guard?

Was one of his farmers working for Darr Gardner? Had one of them told the Rafter Y owner?

'Who in the heck squealed about the meetin', I wonder?'

So Horace Browning had the same devilish thoughts, huh?

'I don't know, Horace. But somebody must've told him.'

'One of the farmers must have mentioned the meeting to somebody. Or else Frances Lacey has shot her big mouth off again. If you want something spread around, jus' tell it to Frances an' swear her to keepin' a secret!'

'Jack told me he'd not tell his wife, though.'

'He might've weakened.'

Browning was right, Buck realized. When too many people knew a secret, then it became anything but a secret. And there was no use in wasting thought on this question. He'd probably never know the answer.

They forded Diamond Willow Creek, got to the benchland, and loped toward the Rafter Y. Buck realized it might have been close to midnight. There was a moon, but clouds kept scuttling in front of it, just allowing an occasional beam of light to seep through, then to be shut off quickly.

The range was in semi-darkness. You could see lines of trees if they were not too far off.

119

The hills, as you got closer, took on form and character, but the light was not sufficient to let you see individual trees and clumps of brush.

Buck figured the night was just about right for the kind of work he and Horace Browning intended doing. Already his mind was running ahead, going to the Rafter Y, building a form of attack.

They would tie their broncs in the buckbrush along Cow Creek, then sneak in from behind the buildings, and then light them. That way the buildings would be between them and the Rafter Y bunkhouse and main buildings. Before the fire was detected, they would be a good two or three miles away, he figured.

'How's your horse, Horace?'

'This easy spell has rested her. An' yours, Buck?'

Buck said, 'He's still tough. We might have to make a fast getaway, and that's why I asked.'

'Yonder's the Rafter Y!'

They drew rein in the buckbrush along Cow Creek. Ahead of them about a quarter-mile were the buildings of the big Gardner ranch.

Buck said, 'This way.'

He followed a trail that led through the brush. They kept their broncs at a walk.

Ahead, an owl hooted. The sound was weird. Its eeriness caused a ball to form in the land locator's belly.

'What was that, Buck?'

Buck listened, and said, 'A hoot owl. And that was the real thing, too. Not a make believe signal.'

The owl hooted again, but this time its cry did not affect Buck because he sort of expected it.

'The real McCoy,' he said.

They rode on, hoofs silent on the damp, rain-soaked soil. Once a bulberry bush's branch came back, hitting the farmer across the face.

Buck murmured, 'Sorry, Horace.'

'You couldn't help it, Buck.'

They rode a few rods further, and here, deep in the buckbrush, Buck drew rein and dismounted, leaving his sorrel with dragging reins. Horace Browning pulled his mare to a halt and followed suit.

'I'd best tie this ol' mare. She ain't rein-busted an' she might try to wander off.'

'Jes' wrap your reins around a big brush,' Buck said. 'Don't tie 'em, 'cause we might have to git out in a heck of a hurry.'

'You got that kerosene?'

'Under my arm.'

'Well, here we goes, eh?'

'Here we go,' Buck agreed.

121

CHAPTER ELEVEN

Buckley Wilson knew that it would take a long time ever to forget this night. That is, if he did ever forget it. For a man always remembers the times he is under the shadow of death.

And that night, death's shadow was strong on him and Horace Browning.

They came to the rim of the brush. About fifty feet away were the Rafter Y buildings they aimed to burn. They were directly behind the old barn, and Buck saw that the rear door was open. The door was not swinging idly in the wind, though; it was strapped back against the barn's wall.

Beyond the barn, just the tip of a gable showing, was the tool shed. Buck hunkered, pulling Horace Browning down beside him.

His voice was a loud whisper.

'So far, no guard. That's good. Here are the buildin's we want to burn. You stay here in the brush and watch for the guard.'

'What do you aim to do, Buck?'

Buck was going to scout through the barn to see no animals were in it. He did not want to burn an innocent horse to death. Browning agreed on this point.

'An' then, Buck?'

'If it has any animals, I'll untie them an' turn them loose. They'll be free then to run out when fire starts eatin' them buildin's.'

'I'll watch close.'

Buck got some matches out of his levi pocket and put them in the breast pocket of his shirt where they would be easier to get at. He gave the strip and the buildings a long, calm look. He spotted nothing that looked like trouble.

Satisfied, he crouched low and ran forward, doubled over the gallon jug of kerosene, the liquid inside making a slight noise. Some of the kerosene had leaked from around the cork. It made a sharp, stinking odor that Buck disliked.

He had some kerosene on his hands, too. He could feel it on his skin.

He stiffened and went down to the ground. Automatically he had his .45 in his hand. He listened, then realized that the owl had hooted again. Still, he was damp across the back, for his shirt seemed to stick to his shoulders. Maybe it was only his imagination, though.

He crouched, a dark ball.

He listened.

Somewhere, a cricket talked, its sound sharp and shrill. The earth was cool and damp

123

and its aroma arose and smelled strong and sharp.

He looked back at the ring of brush, but could not make out the spot where Browning was hidden. A minute dragged slowly by, moving with the reluctant slowness with which time moves while under duress. Then he went ahead again, the kerosene slopping in the jug.

He reached the shadow of the barn and flattened into it, listening. The wind moved through some cottonwood trees, lazy and indifferent, yet holding a certain night chill. His eyes probed here and there, watching, waiting, and hoping no guns would talk from hiding places.

For he knew that guards were out to protect the immense ranch. One of his farmers, while out on the range one day, had watched the Rafter Y through a telescope. He had seen the Gardner men change guards.

So guards were out, he knew.

There was another thing to be considered. That was the element of time. With Browning's house already fired, with the other building in flames, the Rafter Y men would be heading back for the home ranch, their night of infamy through. And he and Horace Browning would have to be out of this vicinity before Gardner and his men returned.

No use inviting odds that were too large, he realized.

He did not hear any animals in the barn. Had there been a bronc or two tied to the stalls he would have heard them move or he would have heard them eating hay. As it was, he heard nothing except the sounds made by the slow wind. And they were small sounds, though they seemed strangely disturbing.

He moved into the barn. Here it was dark and he caught the smell of manure, old and stale, and the odors of hay and oats and of sweat-soaked leather, probably a harness or two or some saddles and saddle blankets.

He listened, standing in the dark. Had there been a beast in the barn he would have smelled him and made some sound. Nevertheless, he went from manger to manger, stopping at last by the wide front door.

No horses in the barn.

He heard a rustle in the haymow, and he realized some doves were up there. He climbed the ladder and came to the mow. Hay was scattered around and he heard a dove cooing overhead. He saw a patch of light at the far end. That meant, then, that the haymow window was open.

When he torched the place, the doves could fly out and be safe.

Moving over the thick hay, he went to the window and looked out. The barn and toolshed were very close together. If the wind came up the fire might even jump to other Rafter Y buildings.

The presence of hay in the haymow changed his plans. He would light the dry hay, scoot down the ladder, then run for Browning and his horse. Then, before the fire had even sent tongues of flame out the haymow window, he and Browning would be miles away.

And, with the fire in the haymow, it would be harder to get at, and therefore harder to put out.

He listened, making sure. There was only the wind in the eaves, and the cooing of the doves. He heaped up a pile of the dry hay and sprinkled it with kerosene. Then, walking across the hay, he let the kerosene trickle out in a line.

He heard the gurgle of the liquid leaving the jug. It came out in spurts. He heard it hit the hay. He walked around in a circle, coming back to where he had started, making a circular line of dampness in the hay.

He stooped, sheltered the match with his palm, then hit it with his thumb. The head flew off, a line of flame that died before it hit the hay. He cursed it silently, and got his second match.

He halted, thumbnail on the match head.

He listened for a full minute.

He thought: I'm getting jumpy. I got to get out of here.

His thumbnail clicked; the match lit. He put it against the kerosene-dampened hay. The fire caught, ran forward; it made a sibilant, sizzling line of fire following the line of the dampness. It made a flame that lighted the interior of the haymow, showing the doves as they flew out the open door.

He waited a precious moment until the entire circle had caught, the fire coming back to its original starting place; then he went down the ladder, swift and fast, for already the fire was strong upstairs.

He ran to the back door, halted there, and he listened.

Upstairs, flames crackled. Outside, doves circled, zoomed. The space between the burning barn and where Horace Browning hid was empty. Gun in hand, he darted across it, running stooped over.

Somewhere, to his side, he heard a sudden, smashing roar, and he knew it was a gun. He saw the blossoming rose of a pistol's flare to his left, coming from a building. He did not hear the sound of the lead.

He figured suddenly that it had gone over

him. He was a dark, compact ball, moving through the darkness.

Somebody hollered, 'Fire, men, an' I shot at a gent.'

The words ended suddenly. The sentence was chopped off abruptly. For Horace Browning was shooting, gun lancing gray flame from the brush. And Buck, too, was flinging shots toward the guard.

Afterwards he did not know how many shots were fired. Horace Browning was firing rapidly, flames blending one into the other, so quickly did his short-gun talk.

Buck fired twice.

They were fast shots, fired as his legs propelled himself across that space. The guard never fired again.

Nor did the guard holler, either.

But the gun roar and the strident yell of the guard had brought the big ranch to life. Somewhere Buck heard men hollering. He figured this was in the Rafter Y bunkhouse.

He didn't waste any time at the Rafter Y.

'Get your horse,' Browning snapped.

Buck smashed through the brush, holstering his gun. He dragged his rifle from scabbard, the move quick and sharp. Snagging his reins, holding both on the left side of his cayuse's neck, he swung into saddle, the rifle rising with him. Already

Browning was riding through the brush.

Men were moving, and somewhere a gun blasted. This brought a quick smile to the land locator's tight lips. Somebody was probably shooting at the ranch cat or dog.

Somebody, he figured, had an itchy trigger finger.

He could not see the flame of the shot, for it came from across the ranch. But he could see the flame spouting out of the barn. The barn, he knew, was doomed. That thought was good in him.

For one precious second, he held his rearing, terrified horse, judging the fire's ferocity. And he knew the Rafter Y men could not put it out. No bucket brigade could quelch that fire with the start it had.

A dove circled, outlined by flickering fire, and then dipped out of sight. Buck thought: The dove of peace, eh?

'Let's drag outa here!'

Browning was rattled. This gave his words a harsh tone. Already he was rowelling across the night, heading out. He was low on his old mare. But Buck did not follow the farmer immediately.

He watched, a cold feeling inside. He hated to destroy property, for property represented work and money, but what other choice had he and Horace Browning? None. You had to fight fire with fire.

He heard men hollering, and he could see their spidery figures, moving against the background of flame. He doubted if pursuit would follow. For one thing, the night was dark, broken only by occasional splotches of moonlight, and a man cannot track in a dark night.

By daylight, the Rafter Y men could trail them, but they would not trail them far, he would see to that. He watched the wind take the flames. Even as he watched, one brand was whipped across space, landing in the new barn that Darr Gardner had built a few years back.

'Save that new barn!'

'Get them buckets of water comin', men.'

He did not hear the voices of either Len Huff or Darrell Gardner. Or, if they were down there, he could not distinguish their voices because of the din and the distance.

Already the new barn was burning. It burned with a fierce conflagration seemingly intent upon destroying itself, it seemed.

He remembered the gun that had spoken out of the dark. He remembered returning its fire, and then the gun had stopped.

Had he or Horace Browning killed a Rafter Y man?

That thought was not good. He didn't like

the taste of it, nor did he like the feel of it. The taste was acrid, bitter to a man's tongue. The feel was rough, and it held no smoothness.

Life, to him, was a precious item. He hated to have been the cause of a man's death. Yet logic came to him, over-flooding sentimentality, and logic said, 'You shot to protect your life, Wilson.'

But there was little, if any, solace in that assumption.

He was sure the man was dead. If he had not been killed would he not have sent other shots towards him, Buck Wilson, and toward Horace Browning? Or had he just fallen, wounded?

Buck Wilson hoped the latter conjecture was correct.

There was nothing he could do by remaining on Rimrock Ridge. The havoc he and Browning had come to do had been brought about.

Up to now, this had been a stalemate war. Now, with these moves, the lid had been ripped loose, and the real issue was at hand. The Rafter Y had demanded its eye and its tooth, and these the outfit had received, but they had in return paid in kind.

Buck spun his bronc, using his spurs.

Horace Browning was waiting along Cow Creek, and he spurred out of the willows. At

131

this moment the moon was up, washing the rangeland with ghostly shadows. Buck caught the reflection of the moon on the man's .45.

'Be careful how you handle that gun, fellow.'

Browning asked, 'What happened, Buck?'

Buck told about the new barn catching on fire. The wind came in suddenly, renewing its energy, whipping his coat out. It would be a foe to the Rafter Y men who fought those flames. It would lift burning brands, swing them in its fingerless grip, and deposit them where it chose.

'Good, Buck.'

Buck said, 'Us for our homes.'

'My home,' said Browning, 'is no more.'

Buck said, 'I'll ride over there with you.'

Browning asked, 'Can they trail us come daylight?' And his voice seemed to hold a quick fear.

'Not if we work it right. Follow me, Horace!'

Already Buck had his sorrel in Cow Creek. Water splashed, water washed against the gelding's forelegs. Behind him came Horace Browning. Browning's old mare splashed with her big hoofs.

Browning said, 'We stopped that guard. I wonder if we killed him?'

Buck did not answer.

They rode a mile in the creek, water splashing, and Browning asked, 'I wonder who that guard was? Wonder what his name was?'

'Who cares?' Buck snapped the words.

Browning was silent then, trailing about ten feet behind Buck. A mile passed, then another. Browning said, 'Far enough, ain't we?'

'About another mile.'

They went this mile, and they were near the headwaters of Cow Creek. The clouds were gone now, but the wind was fierce and Buck found himself wondering if the Rafter Y men had managed to control the fire. Then he realized that the wind was stronger here at this higher altitude.

They had climbed about two thousand feet, he figured. Here there was even snow laced between the pines and spruce. The wind was chilly and he pulled his coat tighter.

They left Cow Creek, and rode through the timber. They came out on a clearing marked by lava and flint and they rode across this with the steel shoes of the broncs making not a scratch against the igneous rock.

'That should throw them off the track,' Browning said.

Buck said, 'They'd never trail this far. The crick did its work.'

133

Buck put the sorrel to a long lope. By the time he got back to his farm on Diamond Willow Creek the morning would be close or maybe with him. Browning put his mare up to Buck's mount.

'We did it, Buck.'

'And it tastes like ashes,' Buck said.

Browning said, 'It sure does.' He considered that, the moonlight across his face, his head cocked. 'Sometimes I think there's no hope for man.'

'Don't say that. Give us the chance.'

Browning said, 'We destroy our chances.'

Buck was in no mood for philosophy. He said, 'Maybe we do,' and let it go at that. To him there seemed some boundaries across which man could not move. This seemed to be one of them.

They crossed a mesa, dotted with scrub pine and juniper, and they reached the level of Porcupine Creek. Buck knew this vast rangeland by heart, for this was his home. He had ridden on roundup with Bar S crews, in those dim, far days that now receded further and further back against the passage of time.

They went down Porcupine Creek with Buck following a trail ground out years before by buffalo. Dawn was dim in the East when they came to the burned-down outfit of Horace Browning.

If at any time Browning cursed it was now. His house was gone, the barn was ashes, his hen house was a dark splotch, his cow had burned in the barn. But what hurt him most was finding his dog, shot through the head.

He held the dog's cold body and looked up at Buck. He tried to speak, but couldn't. He bowed his head and his tears came. Buck said nothing, sitting his bronc, looking at the devastation.

Browning said finally, 'Thanks, Buck.'

Buck said, 'I was glad to help.'

He rode toward Jack Lacey's ranch.

CHAPTER TWELVE

Gardner looked down on the fire and said, 'Well, that's that, although I wished to heck you hadn't killed his dog, Huff.'

Huff sat saddle and studied his boss. Below them the buildings of Horace Browning crackled and sent flame and brands high in the air. Huff thought: He's an odd man. Here he burns down a bunch of buildings an' they don't worry him a bit, but he's worried about a dog I killed.

Huff said, 'He would have bit me. My bullet stopped him like he'd run into a stone

135

wall.'

'He had no stake in this.'

Huff said, 'And I've got no fang holes in my leg. Gardner, there'll be more than that dog kilt, when this is over.'

Gardner watched the fire, the flames etching his rugged face, giving it a reddish tint. He and Huff were in no hurry.

'She'll burn to the ground,' Gardner murmured.

Huff nodded, rolling a smoke.

Gardner said, 'About time them two boys of mine lit that lower barn of Jack Lacey's on fire, ain't it?'

'About time.'

Gardner looked again to the fire below them. The flames coppered the red color of his horse and made the bay look like a bronze statue. The horse stood, ears up, nostrils distended.

'Your bronc smell somethin', Darr?'

Gardner studied his horse's head. 'No, he's just watching the fire, I guess. Well, time we mosey on, eh?'

'Us for the dance, Darr. I can see myself whirlin' that purty schoolmarm aroun', I can. Say, she used to be sweet on you, and now she's almighty leery of you, or so it seems to me.'

'Len, a wild imagination is a bad thing to

136

own.'

Len Huff took the rebuff, his face wooden. They rode along the ridge, the flames making the timber red. Then they topped the ridge, broncs sliding a little in wet shale, and behind them was the red tinge of the fire they had set.

They did not ride fast. Their work was through, and there had been no danger. Even now, there was no danger, for the farmers were all at Buckley Wilson's farm in a meeting.

Huff said, 'Now who tol' you them farmers was at Wilson's, boss?'

Gardner's reply was sour and sarcastic. He did not like to answer questions. 'My little sister told me.'

Huff laughed. 'That's a good one, boss. Your little sister, eh? Why you're too ornery to have any relatives, you are. When you got hatched the're never was another egg like the one that you busted out of!'

'Maybe it was a bad egg.'

Gardner was in a dry, droll type of humor.

'A tough egg,' Huff corrected him.

Gardner said, 'Come on,' and lifted his bay to a lope.

Huff swung in, a pace behind the big Rafter Y owner's horse. And as he rode, Huff realized Gardner had not answered his question. The range boss still did not know who had told Gardner that the farmers would all be at Buck Wilson's. And, plainly, he was curious.

Maybe Darr Gardner and one of the farmers were in cahoots. But Huff, somehow, doubted that line of reasoning. He and Gardner were together most of the time, and had Gardner had a rendezvous with a farmer, then by the law of averages he, Len Huff, should have also witnessed that meeting.

Even now, the fact that Gardner had not told him the name of his confidant was rankling Len Huff. For he was a proud man and his pride demanded he be well informed.

But he did not repeat the question.

Suddenly, Darr Gardner said, 'Look over that-a-way, Len!'

Huff looked, standing on stirrups.

'The boys has torched that Lacey barn,' he said. 'There might be a point in this you've overlooked, Darr.'

'An' that?'

'With only Browning's house burnin', them farmers might've figured the fire was an accident, but with two fires at once they'll be darned certain that the Rafter Y caused them.'

'That's one reason I had two fires at once.'

Huff said, 'You want to pull them against you, huh?'

'That's it.' Gardner was abrupt.

Huff rubbed his jaw. It was still sore from

138

the fist of Buck Wilson. He made no reply. Gardner, it seemed, was always a jump ahead of him.

Gardner said, 'Two nice fires. Well, us for town, an' to whirl the belles aroun', eh?'

Huff said nothing.

They rode another mile or so, taking it easy. If any farmers did come from the Wilson farm to the burning Browning buildings, those farmers would take the short-cut, not ride this trail. Therefore they would not meet them.

The wind was a little chilly, and Len Huff turned on stirrups, aiming to untie his coat that was tied across the cantle of his saddle. This way, he was looking back at the Rafter Y, and therefore he spotted the fire.

'Darr, my Gawd.'

The hoarse, croaking note in his voice made Gardner spin on his bronc, free hand falling to his holstered gun.

'Darr, look!'

For a moment Darr Gardner said nothing. And when he did speak, his voice was normal.

'Them dirty dogs,' he said.

Huff asked, 'An accident?'

Gardner said roughly, 'Use what the Lord gave you for thinkin' with, Huff. Them farmers have outwitted us, I'd say.'

'How?'

'They've sneaked over an' set the Rafter Y

139

on fire. Come on, man, come on! Ride!'

Already the big Rafter Y owner had turned his bay, his spurs working. The bronc streaked down the hill, his rider forgetting all about the dance in town. Huff, cursing wildly, followed, quirt rising.

'You really think they did that?'

'How else would my buildin's git on fire?'

'Well, buildin's burn, don't they?'

'No accident,' Gardner snapped, the wind whipping back his words. 'Make that two-bit cayuse run, Len!'

Len Huff rode hard, pushing his bronc for every ounce he could get out of him, and he knew how to handle a horse, too. But the bay of the Rafter Y boss always was in the lead, a red streak moving across Burnt Wagon Basin. Try though he did, Len Huff could not get his bronc even with the horse of his boss.

Gardner rode low, for when he arched himself over the saddle-horn he made less resistance to the wind. Now and then his quirt worked but he did not need to use the whip on the bay.

He knew the farmers had stolen his thunder. But how they got past his guards he did not know. Maybe his foreman was right. Maybe the fire at the Rafter Y was only an accident.

Logic repeated it was no accident. Despite

his guards and his vigilance, farmers had torched his buildings. But who would expect them to take such an action? Logically, they would have headed for the burning Browning homestead, or to the Jack Lacey barn.

But instead . . .

They crossed Diamond Willow Creek, broncs splashing spray. The far bank was steep and the bay climbed it in great lunging strides, shod hoofs hooking footage. Then, the meadow lands ahead, the bay stretched out again.

Gardner glanced back. Len Huff's horse was just climbing out of the creek. Evidently the bronc had slipped. Gardner held in a little and let Huff catch him.

Huff said, 'My danged bronc fell, boss.'

The moonlight sifted in, showing Huff's clothing, and the mud on them. Gardner figured his range boss had taken a bad tumble, sliding in the mud after his cayuse had gone down.

They came to a ridge, rode along it, and they were about three miles or so from the Rafter Y. The flames had grown, spread by the wind, and Huff panted, 'The ol' barn looks like it's gone. The new one is burnin', too. This thing sure went haywire, Darr.'

'The end ain't in sight!'

They rode across a flat, horses pounding.

Quirts rose and fell, for their broncs were running out of wind. Horseflesh could only stand so much. Gardner pulled in, for he caught a glimpse of two riders, about a quarter of a mile away.

'Who goes there?'

His answer was a rifle ball, singing ahead of him. His own Winchester was out, the lever working. His bronc stood stock-still, trained to a rifle.

Gardner snapped, 'Get them, Huff!'

Huff was shooting, and Gardner's rifle talked, the sounds mixing. But the distance was too far, the night too uncertain. Out yonder rifle flame moved in sudden red bursts. There was, too, the flame of a six-shooter.

Then the two horsemen were gone, drifting into the timber. The night seemed to reach out with dark jaws and grab them. One moment they were in view; the next, they were in the brush.

Gardner jacked a fresh cartridge into his rifle's barrel. The mechanism closed with a sharp click.

'You all right, Len?'

'Never nicked me. An' you?'

'All right.'

Len Huff was cramming cartridges into his magazine. 'Should we trail them, boss?'

142

Darr Gardner shook his head. 'No percentage in that. They'd have all the odds. They could hole up in the rocks an' trick us into riding into an ambush. You got the eyes of a cat, Len. Who was they?'

'Two farmers, I'd say. Who else would shoot at us?'

'I know that.' Gardner was rough. 'But what two farmers?'

'One of them looked like the land locator.' Huff paused, then added, 'But I don't know who t'other one was.'

'One looked like Wilson to me, too.'

Huff put his rifle back into its saddle holster, the leather and steel making a fine sound.

'If thet was Wilson, he was comin' from the Rafter Y, I bet.'

'Maybe it wasn't Wilson.'

'I'm not sure, myself.'

Gardner ordered, 'Ride, Huff,' and his bronc dug out, heading for the Rafter Y.

Again, Huff swung behind. The brief respite had given their broncs a little more wind. They slanted around a bend, bodies ramming into the wind. They hit Cow Creek on the dead run, and their cayuses splashed to the other side.

They broke out of the buckbrush. The burning buildings were in front of them. They

143

felt their heat. Reflection made the buckbrush and cottonwoods and box-elders assume a pinkish tint that looked ghostly against the night.

'Who rides there?'

Both recognized the voice that came from behind them.

'Mac, you such a idiot you don't know your own boss?'

Mac was a short cowboy who toted a rifle.

'Couldn't see you too good ag'in thet fire, Gardner.'

'What happened?' Gardner clipped.

'Somebody lit the ol' barn. The win' took the flames to the new barn. We're fightin' it, but with this wind . . .'

'Who did it?'

'I dunno. But Al Flagg shot at a fellow, I guess.'

'You guess? Don't you know?'

'No, I dunno for sure. You see, Al cain't tell you, either. 'Cause Al Flagg is plumb dead, Al is. He ran roun' the barn, right when they set the fire, an' he stopped a bullet plumb in his chest!'

Darr Gardner's face was as red as a turkey's wattles, and not all of it was reflection from the burning buildings. And this anger was not because the Rafter Y had lost a rider. It was rather because nesters had sneaked in and outwitted a Rafter Y guard, then killed him. The guard, as a man, didn't mean anything. A man could always hire another hand.

Len Huff murmured, 'So they kilt Al, eh?'

'That's right, Len.'

Gardner asked, 'Did Al wound any of them?'

'We cain't fin' no blood in the bresh, Darr. An' this light is so bright a man could see fresh blood, too. Looked like two of 'em, judgin' from the tracks left by their broncs.'

'Whose side did they sneak in on?' he demanded.

'Al's side.'

'Well, can't bawl him out. Come on, Len, we ain't doin' no good here.'

They rode toward the burning buildings. The Rafter Y crew had abolished all efforts to kill the fire by a bucket brigade strung out from the well. The wind had shifted a little and it could not spread the fire to the house.

'Two men,' Len Huff murmured. 'An' we run smack into two riders, Gardner. Too bad we didn't knock them from their horses.'

Gardner had no answer.

The Rafter Y owner rode around the fire, talking to his men who had encircled the building and who were quick to stamp out any brands or sparks that blew from the fire.

'Al Flagg's over there, boss. Under thet

tarp of Smoky's.'

Gardner said, 'Bury him on the hill come daylight.' He did not ride over and look at the dead man. And Al Flagg had come up the trail from Texas with him, too.

He stopped and talked with a dark-skinned cowboy. 'I see you did your chore, Smoky. The barn was on fire, I saw.'

Smoky showed white teeth. 'Easy chore. Not a bit of trouble. That Lacey nester'll have a chore to rebuild his barn. But not as big a chore as the one we have on hand if we aim to build another barn like this one was.'

Gardner had no reply. He had hit, made his move. The farmers had retaliated, and the blame lay on a dead man. He had a feeling his empire was slipping. He had a hunch he'd have to hit soon, and hit hard. But the next time would not be firing a nester's buildings.

The next time, he vowed, he would hit at Buck Wilson.

CHAPTER THIRTEEN

'Hello, the house!'

Buck sat his sweaty bronc and looked at Jack Lacey's house. No lights were in the windows and that, he thought, was odd. But

146

maybe Jack and Frances were down at the other end of their homestead, fighting the fire that was consuming their lower barn.

Buck loped over the hill, and came to the burning barn. By now the fire was very low, the barn a victim to its flames.

'Buck Wilson comin' in!'

He waited for a reply, but caught none. So he rode openly up to the barn, repeating, 'Buck Wilson comin' in!'

A short search showed him the Laceys were not in the vicinity. This brought a frown to Buck as he sat with one leg slung over the saddle-horn and rolled a cigarette. The Laceys were not at home. They were not down here at their burning barn, either. Then where were they?

Something cold and hard fastened its icy fingers around his belly. Frances Lacey had been at home, alone, and her husband had attended the meeting on Diamond Willow Creek. Had something happened to Frances while Jack Lacey had been gone?

Logic pushed this thought aside. He was sure that even Darr Gardner knew better than to cause trouble with a nester's woman, be she his wife or daughter. Gardner knew that this basin and its inhabitants would not tolerate such actions, even from the Rafter Y men.

Where, then, were the Laceys?

Buck rode back to the farmhouse. But it was deserted. The door was unlocked, and he went inside and lit the lamp and found nothing. Then he went to the barn back of the house.

A match's flare showed him no saddles were in the barn. A work team looked at him from a stall, eyes wide in the match light.

He killed the match.

He considered the matter of time that had elapsed since the dismissal of the farmers from the meeting at his farm. He and Browning had ridden to the Rafter Y, made a wide circle, and then he had left Browning and ridden to this farm. Quite a bit of time had passed.

He rode to his farm. He came in calling, 'Buck comin', Hatchet Joe!'

The Chinese came out of the buckbrush. 'Me hear you come. Fire over that way!' He pointed to the Rafter Y and lower barn on the Lacey homestead.

Buck told him about firing the Rafter Y outfit. Hatchet Joe had a chuckle as dry as two sticks rubbing together.

'You seen Jack Lacey?'

'Me no see him. Why you ask, Buckley boy?'

Buck told him.

Hatchet Joe said, 'Maybe his wife she go to the dance tonight. When he leave here he tell
148

me mebbeso she go. She mad at him when he left, so he say. He wonder if she be home when he come.'

'She must have rid into town, an' when he come home an' found the house empty, I reckon he jes' rid in after her, eh?'

'No fin' nobody aroun' the barn that burn?'

Buck shook his head.

'Then they in town, Buck. No know their barn, she burn.'

Buck said, 'I'll get a fresh bronc an' ride into town. I'd best tell them about their barn bein' burnt down.'

Hatchet Joe chuckled, and this time his chuckle had mirth.

'What're you grinnin' about, you tame ape?'

'You no wanta see Lacey, mebbeso? You all the time want to see Laura an' mebbeso that purty girl Martha?'

Buck said, 'Go on your way, you ol' schemer!'

'Me, I stay in bush, an' guard.'

Buck got a fresh horse from the barn and changed saddles.

When he got to town the dance was in full swing. Even before he got to the dance hall he could hear the sawing of the fiddle and the calls of the squaredance caller.

These country dances sometimes became

149

wild affairs. Whiskey was not scarce and sometimes it flowed too freely and fists started flying. That was another reason he was coming to the dance, he told himself.

If Jack Lacey and his wife had ridden into town, there might be some Rafter Y hands at the dance; Lacey might get into a fight. And he'd be one lone farmer against a number of Gardner hands.

He had a sort of big-brother feeling for Lacey.

A man said, 'Well, Buck himself. Have a drink, Buck?'

'Not now, Clayton.'

'Won't last long, Buck.' Clayton hung onto his arm in a drunken manner. He swamped in the Cinch Ring Saloon.

Buck took a drink to get rid of the old drunk. But he made it a short drink; so short, in fact, that Clayton, in a generous mood, demanded he take another. But to this the land locator did not consent.

Clayton followed him a few paces, bottle outstretched, then turned and went to another townsman, who sat drunkenly against a cottonwood tree, not caring whether the dance kept on or instantly stopped.

Buck stood in the hallway, studying the crowd. And he could not see a single Rafter Y man. This brought a grim smile to his lips.

The Rafter Y men had been too busy setting fires to attend. Now they were too busy trying to put out a fire on their own ranch.

He doubted if anybody in this hall knew about the fires on this range, except for the Laceys. And look though he did, he could not see the couple.

This dance had started early and trees surrounded the hall, shutting off the view of the burned buildings. Yes, and the high ridge north of town also would be a barrier preventing a view of the blazes.

The Laceys, he decided, were not in the dance hall. Not one of his farmers was in attendance. That was justifiable. They were home guarding their properties.

He saw Laura first. The dark-haired little school teacher was dancing with a member of the school board, heavy-set Jocko Overly, who ran the blacksmith shop. Overly, he remembered, was the chairman of the school board.

Laura was playing her cards close to her chest, he decided. But then it came to him that she always played her own brand of politics.

She saw him and nodded, her eyes telling things that the nod hid.

Buck nodded, then looked for Martha. He saw her over on the other side of the hall talking with Mrs. Overly. He went to the ticket seller and said, 'Here's my buck.'

'Too late, Buck. Only an hour or two left. We quit sellin' tickets at midnight.'

Buck smiled. 'Lucky for once, Harold.' He started toward Martha, stopped and asked, 'Were the Laceys here tonight?'

'Not that I seen, Buck. None of your farmers has been in here.'

Buck nodded, still wondering. Had Jack and Frances gone over to spend the night with one of their neighbors? That wasn't logical, he decided. Jack Lacey was no coward to begin with. He would not run to a neighbor for protection.

Lacey would fight for his property.

Martha said, 'Well, so you made it here, huh?'

'In the flesh.' Buck bowed to Mrs. Overly. 'May I have this dance, madam?'

'Oh, pshaw, go on, Buck. You're jest bein' polite. You came to dance with Martha, not me.'

Martha was in his arms. Martha, warm and satisfying. Her blonde hair was against his chin, her delicate perfume a spicy aroma.

'How come you're a wallflower?'

She did not look up. 'I thought you'd be along soon. So I sat out that dance, even though Tony Martinelli wanted me to dance

152

with him.'

Buck said, 'Ouch.'

She looked up, her eyes serious. 'What's the matter?'

'An apron string,' Buck said. 'I felt it fasten around me.'

Her head went down, nestled against him. 'Apron strings are only made out of cloth. They're not hard to break.'

'That,' said Buck, 'is what you think.'

Laura and Mr. Overly danced by, and Overly nodded at Buck rather coldly. He was also one of the townspeople who refused to get wised-up. Buck knew that since the farmers had come the blacksmith's income had more than doubled. Prior to the coming of the farmers the blacksmith had been in dire straits.

For the Rafter Y did most of its own blacksmith work out on the ranch. Occasionally one of the cowboys would get Overly to shoe a horse and once in a while Darr Gardner would shove an occasional welding job onto the Burnt Wagon smithy.

But the Rafter Y had not had him sharpen and point plowshares. Nor had he repaired machinery—farming machinery—for the Gardner spread. Time had been when Overly sat in the shade and yarned. Now he frequently worked late at night, sounds of his

153

hammer floating across town.

But still he gave just a cold nod to Buck.

Laura scowled, and said, 'Hello, Buck.'

'Howdy, schoolmarm.'

They danced on and Buck said, 'She didn't speak to you, Martha. You two got a hen on?'

'Nonsense! We had a long talk earlier in the evening. You don't think we'd fight over such a useless man as you, do you?'

'Why, thank you, honey.'

'Now close your mouth and keep dancing.'

Some of the tension left Buckley Wilson. The music was not the best in the world, but what it lacked in rhythm was made up for by its loudness. The pianist pounded, cheeks high with drink and the heat of the hall, and the fiddler sawed and sawed, and sometimes they happened both to be on the same measure.

Buck asked, 'Did you dance with Jack Lacey?'

'Jack Lacey? You mean the farmer?'

'None other. Only man by that name on this range.'

'He hasn't been to the dance.'

'See his wife?'

'Two days ago she was in the store.'

'No, I mean tonight.'

She looked up, eyes puzzled. 'I don't follow your conversation one bit. Mr. Lacey has not

154

been at this dance that I know of. Therefore it stands to reason his wife has not been here, doesn't it?'

'You can't tell about these women nowadays,' Buck grunted. 'Some of them seem to like to run off to a dance an' leave the ol' man t'home with the young ones. These modern women are hard critters to understan' sometimes.'

'My great-great-grandfather said that, too,' she said caustically. 'I don't think you need to worry about Mrs. Lacey. She adores her husband. You can see it every time she looks at him.'

'I never saw it.'

'You men can't see the things a woman sees.'

Buck said, 'Thank heaven for that.'

'You're a case, Buckley.'

Buck said nothing more. When she used the word *Buckley* he knew he was in hot water. She had acquired that habit from his mother. For when Mrs. Charlie Wilson had said to her son, 'Now Buckley,' then her son knew she was angry.

This had started out all right, but his tongue had got twisted some way. He didn't just know where he had made the verbal slip but he knew definitely he had made one.

'You're a cute little trick, Martha.'

155

'Don't try to josh me.'

Buck said, 'Let's get married.'

'Seems to me you said that rather jokingly. I'll bet you've said the same thing to Laura many times. How was her rock collection?'

Buck groaned.

They danced, both silent.

Buck asked, 'Who told you?'

'It's all over town. You stopped at the school house on your way out of town yesterday. You were in the building a little over four minutes.'

'How much over?'

'A few seconds. Old Maid Chesterton watched from her upstairs window and she timed you. Now, there you are, Buckley.'

Buck said, 'Wonder if her clock was accurate?'

'Makes no difference to me,' Martha said airily.

The dance finally ended. Buck escorted her to the bench and bowed and thanked her. Her eyes, he noticed, were laughing. He didn't like their silent laughter. He went outside and took a big drink from the closest bottle, and there were quite a few close ones.

'Gettin' any better, Buck?'

'Heck, I'm not sick.'

'You gotta be sick,' the bottle owner insisted. 'Any man that'd be foolish enough to rush two women like you're doin' has to be sick—above the head. Another drink, Buck?'

'Not out of your bottle.'

The man laughed and tilted his bottle. Buck went into the hall. The man's words burned worse than the home-distilled whiskey.

Two women, huh?

Now how did these people get that way? He wasn't chasing the two women. They were chasing him. Couldn't people see their hands in front of their noses?

But a man always got all the blame. His father had always claimed that a man chased a woman until *she* caught him. But that was wrong in this case, too. He wasn't doing the chasing.

The music started again, the fiddle off tune. Although he knew Martha Buckman was looking at him, he crossed the hall and bowed in front of Laura Fromberg, who was sitting on the bench.

'Dance, Laura?'

'Yes, Buck.'

They glided away. Buck glanced at Martha. Her chin up, she was slipping into Mr. Overly's fat arms.

'Thought you'd eventually get here, Buck.'

'Better late than never.' That was the first thing he could think of.

She sighed, and nestled her dark head

157

against his chest. 'Dancing with that Mr. Overly is like dancing with an elephant.'

'Never have tried that.'

Her head arose again at his terse voice.

'What's the matter, Buck?'

'Nothin'.'

He was sure not a soul in this hall knew about the three fires that had marred this once peaceful range. Had anybody known about them they would have mentioned them to him by this time.

He had finally decided that the Laceys had gone over to the Shermans' farm. Frances Lacey had hen-pecked her husband into going to their neighbors' farm, claiming she had been afraid.

'What are your thoughts, Buck?'

Buck said, 'I was thinkin' of you, Laura.'

'You were! Well, now what were you thinking?'

'Golly, I forgot.'

Her eyes probed his rather boldly. 'I haven't forgotten yesterday afternoon at the schoolhouse, Buck.'

'Get away from me, apron string!'

Her head went down and he knew that she was shamming hurt.

'Buck, how can you say such things?'

'With my tongue, of course.'

'Oh, well, I'll get you, if I want you. But

158

maybe I don't want you. Ever think of that?'

'The thought,' said Buck, 'has never occurred to me.'

The dance ended. Buck bowed and turned to go and a man was at his elbow. 'Buck, I want to see you outside.'

Buck joked, 'Want to fight me, Ike?'

'Nope, not you. I pick my victims. But I got to tell you something, Buck, in private.'

Laura asked, 'Something wrong?'

Buck said, 'Not a thing. Ike here has a bottle he wants me to sample, that's all. Thanks again, Laura.'

'I'll see you again.'

'Maybe.'

Laura was scowling. Buck saw her glance at Martha. The eyes of the two girls met, and Laura suddenly lost her scowl.

'See you, Buck.'

Laura made her voice loud enough so that it carried to Martha. For that matter, the rest of the hall heard it, also.

Buck found his face reddening. He followed Ike outside, wondering what was on the man's mind.

Ike stopped under a tree.

'Buck, I was downtown a minute ago. Had a bottle cached in the alley an' I went after it.'

'Thanks,' Buck said, 'but I've had enough licker for tonight.'

'I ain't offerin' you a drink, unless you wants one. But here I was, diggin' under that big trash can looking for my bottle. For a while I thought I'd lost it, or somebody had seen me cache it an' had stole it.'

Buck felt the push of impatience. He had had a hard night. He noticed that dawn was coming, making trees assume individualities, showing the rigs and teams and saddle horses tied around the hall.

The eastern hills were gathering shadows from the light.

'Nobody'd stole it, though. I found it an' . . .'

'What's behin' this, Ike? Chop it short.'

Ike did. Two riders had come down the alley, and behind Doc Crow's office one had fallen from his bronc.

'I helped wake up Doc. Lord, he's a sound sleeper. But Frances Lacey is in his office now . . .'

'Frances Lacey?'

'Yep, somebody done shot her. Her husband took her into town. Doc sent me for you.'

But Buck was already running toward Doc Crow's office.

CHAPTER FOURTEEN

Jack Lacey had been taking off his boots when he had seen the fire the Rafter Y men had set.

'Fran, the barn, it's burnin' up!'

His wife sat upright in bed, staring out the window. Jack was already pulling on his boots. He ran to the corner, grabbed his Winchester .30-30, and she heard him slam cartridges into the barrel and magazine.

'Jack, that barn had no reason to catch on fire!'

'Somebody lit it, jus' like they lit Brownin's house!'

'Jack, where you going?'

'I'm going out there with this rifle. There might be a chance that one of the Rafter Y men thet burned it is still around.'

'They won't be there, Jack. That fire has burned for some time and you just happened to notice it. They've done their work and they've gone already.'

'I might find one.'

He ran out the door, cramming cartridges into his pockets. She heard him run into the barn and she knew that he was going to get a saddle horse. The flames of the burning barn were dying a little, she thought.

She thought, 'I'd best go with him,' and she got out of bed, hurriedly dressing in levis and a flannel shirt and riding boots. While she sometimes nagged her husband, she was a good woman at heart, and her nagging came out of her worry for his safety. She pulled on her shoes and got a pistol from the dresser drawer.

She knew how to shoot it, too. Jack had showed her how and, while she was not much for accuracy, she was not too bad with the short-gun. She came running to the barn just as he led out his saddled horse.

'Wait for me, Jack.'

'You stay home!'

'I'll not stay home. You're not bossing me around! I'm not having you ride down to that barn and ride into an ambush!'

'There won't be no ambush.'

'Just the same, I'm going with you.'

He held his bronc, waiting for her to saddle. From the height of his saddle he could see the fire more clearly and he saw that the barn was almost down. She was right. There was no hurry.

He said, 'We circle it first, Fran.'

'Good idea.'

They headed out, circling the burning building, but they found no Rafter Y men around it. Finally, their search complete, they rode boldly down to the fire. By this time the barn was only a bunch of hot coals that winked and blinked as the wind fanned them.

Then he saw another fire and he said, 'Look at that, Fran.'

She saw it, too. She turned in saddle, hands braced against fork and cantle, and finally she said, 'That fire is at the Rafter Y, isn't it?'

'Sure looks that way to me,' he admitted.

She studied the fire and then she scowled. 'Now that makes three fires. Our barn, Browning's property, and now this fire at the Rafter Y. Now who do you suppose set that fire?'

'I sure don't know. Browning and Buck rode for Browning's farm an' the rest of us hoemen went home. This don't make sense to me.' Jack Lacey looked back at his burned-down barn. 'That barn cost me over a hundred bucks, not to mention our labor, an' them dirty sons torched it down!'

She looked at her husband. For the first time she noticed the signs of middle-age creeping in his face, and she also noticed that his face was very hard. She had never seen him that angry before.

'We'll rebuild it, Jack.'

He said, 'We ride a wide circle, Frances. We might run into them that set this fire.'

They swung to the west. They rode through

buckbrush and across flats, and at the Rafter Y the flames lifted. There was much here that Jack Lacey did not understand. The chief question was: Who had put fire to the Rafter Y? Or had the fire started of its own accord, an accident?

Suddenly his wife said, 'Riders coming, Jack.'

They came out of the night, two riders drifting across the moonlight. They rode hard, hitting for the Rafter Y. Lacey caught the rise and fall of a quirt, heard the hard pounding of their hoofs on the earth.

Suddenly, one rider cried out something, and guns were in their fists. Lacey heard the high whine of a bullet and his own rifle was talking, the hammer rising and falling. He could not see them well enough for positive identification, but he was sure they were Darr Gardner and Len Huff.

Beside him, he heard the yammer of the pistol in his wife's hand, and a sort of dogged pride arose in him. She was a brave woman. Most women would have turned their broncs and they would have run, but not Frances Lacey.

Jack Lacey jacked a new cartridge into the barrel of his rifle, the mechanism making a loud click. The riders were gone now, drifting into the night. The hills hid them—even the rattle of their hoofs was lost as distance came in.

Lacey leaned on his stirrup and looked at his wife. 'Fran, that was them two Rafter Y men. That was Gardner an' Huff. Frances, what's the matter, honey?'

'My side, Jack.'

She was slipping down into her saddle, and then he was on foot holding her into leather. She caught herself and straightened a little, the moonlight showing her tiny, pained smile.

'They shot you, honey?'

There was fear in his voice. A hesitant, awful fear.

'My right side.'

He moved around the horse and looked at her side. Blood had come out to stain her flannel shirt. The fear in him was now mingled with a great anger. He had never been so angry before. But yet never had he been so calm, either.

'We'll have to get you to town.'

Her hands made explorations. Finally she said, 'The bullet went right through. If I had something to pack it with to keep it from bleeding . . .'

His shirt was off and being ripped into strips. He handed her the strips and asked, 'Could I help, Fran?'

'Yes, Jack.'

He lifted her shirt and then lit a match and looked at the wound. Her skin was ivory and smooth above the bullet-holes, but below it was marked by the stickiness and darkness of blood. The wound itself was small, a little more than a hole that could be left by a sharp match; it bubbled a little.

'Are you bleeding inside?'

'I don't think so.'

He said, 'We'll bandage it as good as we can. Then we can get a buckboard from the farm and I can take you into Doc or go in after Doc. We'll see how you feel when we get home.'

He bound the wound, running the strips around her small waist, and he held his head down so she could not see the naked horror of his eyes. When he was done she sighed and said, 'I didn't know you were that good as a doctor.'

'Good girl,' he said, and mounted his bronc.

They rode toward home and he rode close to her. She seemed stronger, and she said the first shock of the bullet had passed. They got home and she said she wanted to ride right on into town on horseback.

He felt like debating that point and putting her in the buggy. Then he decided to let her have her own way, for surely she knew her

166

own physical strength.

Later he would regret this decision.

The distance from their farm to Burnt Wagon town was a little over five miles. Never had he known that five miles could be so long in time and distance. About two miles from their Diamond Willow Creek farm she slipped in her saddle suddenly, almost falling to the ground.

Luckily, he was riding close to her. He caught her in time. Her saddle horse was old and well trained and he stood like a rock while Jack Lacey held his wife. Her head was on his shoulder and he thought, for a while, she had suddenly died.

This thought, at first, was wild, desperate and terrible, and he knew that if she had died, he would ride with his gun to the Rafter Y. Then her head moved and her breath was soft on his neck.

'I'm sorry, Jack.'

'You almost passed out.'

'I guess I did.'

He held her for a while, kissing her on the cheek, and her strength returned. But still, their broncs standing shoulder to shoulder, he kept his arm around her, waiting for her to declare herself strong enough to ride again.

'Frances, we're getting out of this blasted country.'

'Oh, no, we're not. My mind is made up to that. They can't run me off, even though one of them did shoot me. But we're not sure those two were Gardner and Huff, are we?'

'No, they were too far away.'

'We're not going, Jack.'

He patted her hair, his hands clumsy. He himself did not want to go. They had nothing to return to in the East. All they had—what little they had—was in this Burnt Wagon country.

And most of that was *hope*.

His chief desire in life was to strike back at the Rafter Y. If his wife died . . . He looked at the stars and said a silent prayer. She couldn't die. Just a few minutes ago she had been well and strong and then that little piece of steel-jacketed lead had punctured her side and now . . .

'I can ride, Jack.'

'Are you sure?'

'Yes, I'm sure.'

'Maybe it's best you lie down on the ground and I'll lope into town for Doc Crow and a buggy and come out after you.'

'How far is it to town?'

'About three miles.'

'I can ride that.'

He looked at her pale, sweet face. 'All right,' he said at length, 'but I'll ride almighty
168

close to you at all times.'

'That'll be nice, Jack.'

They rode at a walk, for he knew a trot or gallop would be beyond her ability. Their broncs were well-broken and old to the saddle and this was in their favor. The horses moved along, very close together.

Jack Lacey had his right hand on her hand as it hung to the saddle-horn. He talked to give her strength and to take her mind off her wound and her pain. He talked of Ohio and the moonlight there, but when she replied her voice held no homesickness.

Her voice was clear and strong.

'The moon here is prettier, Jack.'

He talked then of their homestead. How they would rebuild the barn, how the land would yield good crops, how he would build her a new house when they had their first crops, and she would have that sink in it she wanted, and he would build a dam in the creek and she would have water piped into her kitchen.

'We could pipe it into the barn, too, for the water trough. Then the cows wouldn't have to leave the barn in the winter to get to water.'

'Good idea.'

The talk was small and, to most people, it would have proven very tiring, but to them it meant much, for they would work together side by side. The horses plodded, moving toward the town that seemed, mile by mile, to move itself further down the trail.

But he had to keep up her spirits.

'Another mile, Frances.'

'How can you tell?'

'There is the corner of a section line. See the iron stake over there? You can barely see it in the night. Over by that big sagebrush.'

'I think I see it.'

He went on to explain about survey lines. First, surveyors made a meridian, which was a common meeting point. They worked both sides of this, putting in townships. A township was six miles by six miles, and therefore was composed of thirty-six sections.

'Money from two of those sections in each township goes to upkeep and operation of the public schools. Those sections are numbered eighteen and thirty-six. That's a school section right north of our place.'

'Oh, so that's why it is called a school section, huh?'

'That's it.'

Her head was down now, but her body was still stiff, he noticed. He found himself praying that the distance could be, by some superhuman effort, chopped down and shortened.

But the earth, and the moon, were

impassive.

'When a person is in pain, she thinks of lots of things, Jack. But the thing that seems the most awful is that man always wants to put pain onto other men. I wonder why?'

'He's greedy all the time, Fran.'

'Sometimes he's a beast.'

Lacey had no answer to this.

She said, 'You know, Jack, I've been thinking about that fire at the Rafter Y. I'm sure Buck set it.'

'I've been wonderin' about that, too.'

'He could have done it. Instead of heading for Browning's farm he and Horace might have gone to the Rafter Y. That explains why Darr Gardner and Len Huff were riding so fast, heading for home, when they shot me.'

'That's right Fran. They might have been heading for the dance tonight, then seen the fire, then turned back, which would explain how we happened to meet. That all seems logical to me, too.'

'Wonder if Buck and Horace got hurt? Gardner and Huff might have jumped them, you know.'

'I don't know. But Buck can take care of himself. Did you ever see him shoot his pistol?'

'Once.'

'He can draw fast, and shoot straight. But

Horace—well, he's no gunman, he ain't.'

There was a silence.

Jack Lacey thought: We're about a quarter of a mile from town.

Frances asked, 'What was that sound?'

He recognized the sound of the violin and the piano and said, 'That comes from the dance. Here, we'll ride down this alley. It runs behind Doc Crow's office. Almost there, honey.'

A man came out of the shadows and said, 'This is Ike Maloney. Somethin' wrong? Oh, it's you, huh, Jack!'

'My wife has been shot, Ike.'

'Shot? An accident? Hey, she's fallin'! I'll catch her, Jack. Now you get off your hoss an' help me on this side, eh?'

They got Frances Lacey to the ground and they carried her to the back door of Doc Crow's office. They set her down on the steps, and while Jack Lacey held his wife, Ike Maloney pounded on Doc Crow's door.

'Is he in, Ike?'

'I think so. He's a sound sleeper. Oh, Doc, wake up! Hey, Doc!' Ike pounded and kicked on the door. 'Wake up, Doc Crow!'

'Don't rip down the door, you ornery drunk.'

Jack Lacey said, 'This is Jack Lacey, Doc. My wife has been shot.'

The door popped open. Doc Crow stood in baggy underwear.

'Bring her in, an' I'll light a lamp.'

But Ike Maloney had already lighted the lamp. Doc Crow and Jack Lacey carried the unconscious woman into the office where they put her on her back on the high table.

Jack Lacey said, 'Doc, you got to save her, Doc!'

Doc said, 'I'll do my darndest, Jack.'

Ike asked, 'Anything I can do, Jack?'

'Buck Wilson at the dance?'

'He was jes' a minute ago. I jes' come from there. Had a bottle cached down in this alley an' I was jes' getting it when you two come. Here, take a snort of it, 'cause you look like you need it.'

Jack Lacey drank and Doc Crow drank; then the bottle was returned to Ike Maloney. Doc Crow looked down at the unconscious woman, his finger taking her pulse count, his eyes meeting Jack Lacey's.

'Pulse strong. She hasn't lost too much blood.'

'A man never knows how much he loves a woman until he's in danger of losing her,' Lacey told the world in general. 'Ike, go down an' get Buck for me, will you?'

'Sure will, Jack.'

173

CHAPTER FIFTEEN

Buckley Wilson said, 'So you're not sure just who shot at you? Is that it, Jack?'

'Two riders,' Jack Lacey replied. 'Came driftin' outa the night, saw us an' their guns popped.' He shook his head. 'I figure they were Rafter Y men, an' they looked like they was maybe Darrell Gardner an' Len Huff.'

'Could you swear to that on a witness stand?'

'Well, not honestly, no.'

Buck said, 'No evidence, then. The finger points to the Rafter Y, but it doesn't pin any two men down for sure.'

'Maybe this won't get into court, Buck.'

Buck said, 'Play your cards close, fellow. Don't tell nobody what you told me. Just keep your two lips buttoned. This is a dangerous game, and the less a man shoots off his mouth, the better off he is.'

'Okay, Buck, but if I runs into Gardner or Huff, it'll be trouble. 'Cause I know danged well them two was behind this. If it wasn't them thet burned down my barn, it was on orders of the Rafter Y. If it weren't them thet shot at us, then it was two of their riders. Them riders work for Huff an' Gardner. That lays the blame on their shoulders, to my way of thinkin'.'

Buck nodded. He went across the room to where Doc Crow bent over Frances Lacey. His eyes asked a question.

'Steel-jacketed bullet, Buck. Ran through the side of her stomach wall but didn't pierce an intestine, I don't think. All I can do is open the wound a little, then check it, and close it.'

Buck nodded.

Jack Lacey, seated on the bench along the far wall, heard and nodded, too.

Buck asked, 'Do you need help? You'll have to use ether, won't you?'

Doc Crow nodded. 'Get Martha Buckman.'

Buck went outside. The dance had broken up, spirit leaving the dancers when they heard about a woman being shot. Men and women were moving toward their homes, and a buckboard went down the street, ghostly against the dawn, heading for some far outlying ranch.

'May I help, Buck?'

Laura Fromberg stood in the shadows, talking to a townsman. Martha Buckman stood to one side talking with Mrs. Overly.

'Doc wants you, Martha.'

'All right, Buck.'

Martha went into the doctor's office. Buck saw a quick frown come across Laura's face

175

and then as quickly disappear. It seemed as if he had always had to make a decision between the two.

Laura asked, 'Is she hurt badly, Buck?'

Her teeth were chattering from the cold of the northern dawn. Buck looked down into her dark eyes.

'Not too bad, Laura. Doc says he can pull her through.'

'Who shot her?'

'Don't know for sure, Laura.'

Her eyes told him that she did not believe his falsehood. 'Probably some of the Rafter Y outfit, I suppose.'

'Might be,' Buck returned.

A man came up the alley and the land locator recognized him as a Rafter Y man. Evidently he had been playing poker over in the Cinch Ring Saloon.

'I'd head for home if I was you, Cotter.'

Cotter stopped and looked at him. 'An' why, sodbuster?'

Cotter's tone held a contemptuous note that drove anger through Buck Wilson. This night had been a long and hard one.

'Frances Lacey got shot. She's in Doc Crow's office now, Cotter. Her husband thinks some of the Rafter Y men shot her.'

'Everything blamed on my outerfit, eh? Them sodbusters cain't handle a gun.

Mebbeso she shot herself, eh?'

A man said, 'Cotter, ride out. You're purty drunk.'

'The devil with you, MacPherson. I've stood enough of this slurrin' ag'in' my outerfit. These sodmen think they own this earth an' us cowpokes is mud under their brogans.'

Buck said, 'Should I hit him?'

'Some other time,' Laura said. 'He's been drinking, Buck.'

Buck looked at the cowpuncher. They measured each other in silence. Cotter had his hand hooked in his gunbelt right ahead of his .45. All he had to do was jerk back his hand, let his fingers fasten around the grip, and the gun would come up in one continuous motion.

Buck met his gaze with a cold steadiness. He had never liked the arrogant cowpuncher. Cotter always hung around town and the land locator had often wondered if the cowboy were not a spy for Gardner and Huff. Cotter never punched cows or rode bog. Most of the time he stuck around the Cinch Ring.

Buck said, 'Get your horse and ride for home.'

'Can you make me?'

A voice said, 'I can make you go, Cotter.'

Buck had been watching Cotter's right hand and had not noticed Jack Lacey come out of

177

the medico's office.

Cotter turned and said, 'Try it, Lacey; try.'

Lacey was savage, and his fist rose with a savage fury. It chopped Cotter's words short, breaking them off sharp.

Cotter went back. Buck stepped forward and put his arm around the man, pinning the other's arms. He had his hand on Cotter's gun.

Cotter gasped, 'Lemme go, sodbuster!'

Lacey stood, fists knotted, fists down. His face was pale and pulled with anger. Buck still hung onto Cotter.

Buck asked, 'Fists or guns, Lacey?'

'I'm no gunman. Fists.'

Buck had Cotter's .45. He stepped back. Cotter asked angrily, 'I get no choice, huh?'

'Nobody gave Frances Lacey a choice,' Buck reminded him coldly.

Cotter studied him, and Lacey moved closer. Suddenly Cotter turned, right fist moving as his body pivoted, and that right smashed into Jack Lacey's face. It did not move Lacey. Nothing could move Lacey this night.

Lacey took it, and Buck saw the blood start from the farmer's nose. Cotter hit again and this missed, and Lacey went to work. Buck had never guessed that the slim farmer had so much strength or precision.

Lacey was a machine—a fighting machine.

Cotter could fight, too. He'd seen his share of barroom brawls. He used all the dirty tactics that years of rough-and-tumble fighting had taught him. He used them all, and used them savagely, but they were not enough. He was in the wrong and Jack Lacey was in the right.

Maybe that had something to do with it, Buck thought. Maybe when a man fought for the right, he was more powerful. Maybe when a man believed in his convictions, his fight to defend them was stronger.

Buck watched fascinated, yet sick inside. He could feel Laura's fingers clutching his arm, and once he was aware of her saying, 'Stop it, Buck, please! Stop it, or he'll kill Cotter!'

'Let 'im kill 'im!'

'Buck!'

It wasn't too one-sided. Cotter saw to that. Once he knocked Jack Lacey down with a sledge-hammer blow to the belly. Buck thought Lacey would be knocked out. Cotter rushed in to kick the farmer. But Lacey rolled over, cat-quick. Cotter's boot missed and Lacey snagged the man's ankle. A quick, hard jerk and Cotter went down. His boot left his foot, and Lacey threw it to one side as he got up.

'Get up an' fight, cowpuncher!'

Cotter sprang up, but Buck noticed he was not as quick in getting to his feet as Jack Lacey had been. Cotter came up from all fours and they met. They stood and slugged, all science forgotten, both wrapped in a cold fury. The sounds of their fists were loud.

Men watched, knowing they would never see a more desperate fight. Buck felt Laura's fingers grip his arm again and he moved to one side, but she went with him. This fight had run all of five or six minutes, he figured.

It couldn't last much longer.

Both men, he saw, were getting winded. He could hear their heavy breathing—the sharp, sickening sound as they gulped air. Their fists were probably as heavy as lead now, he realized.

Cotter was the first to break. And he broke back only because Jack Lacey's fists drove him back. The cowpuncher caught himself, teetered on his heels, and for a moment his guard was down.

And Jack Lacey used that moment's advantage.

His fists came in, working with renewed effort. They smashed into Cotter's belly, doubling him; they rose upward, savage and fierce with upper-cuts. Cotter hung against space, head back; then he crumpled in the alley, knocked cold.

Buck came in, caught Lacey's arms, pinning them. The man was out on his feet, fighting from instinct. He twisted, cursed.

'Lemme go!'

Buck held him. 'He's down, Lacey! He's knocked cold.' To a townsman, 'Get him outa here, Carl. Pete, help Carl get that cowboy on his bronc. Get him out of town or there'll be a killin'.'

'Okay, Buck.'

The two men picked up Cotter, one at his head, the other at his feet. Cotter was a limp bag of sawdust between them, back sagging. They went up the alley toward the livery barn.

By this time Jack had stopped his struggling.

'I'll be good, Buck.'

Buck released him. The man turned and his face was not nice to look at there in the dawn.

'I whipped the son, Buck?'

'You gave him a good beatin'.'

Lacey smiled twistedly. 'Wish he'd been Huff or Gardner, though. No use me wastin' that much fight on a hired hand of Gardner's.'

'He asked for it,' Buck reminded him. 'If you hadn't cleaned him I would have. Though I doubt if I could have done as good a job as you did, Jack.'

Sanity returned to Jack Lacey. 'Lord, what

will Frances think of me, fightin' in an alley like a thug?'

'I think she'll be right proud of you, Jack.'

For the first time Lacey saw the gun in Buck's right hand. 'Whose gun?'

'Cotter's.'

Lacey nodded. 'Oh.' He started for the medico's office. 'Reckon I'd best wash my mug, eh?'

Laura and Buck were the only people left in the alley. The dawn was brighter and it reflected from her dark hair. She was a lovely picture, dark and small in her party dress with its gay bunch of flowers on the shoulder.

Her eyes were serious and her voice was worried. 'Oh, Buck, where will this end, and how?'

Buck shrugged and spread his hands in a gesture of puzzlement. 'Heaven only knows, Laura. But it looks to me like there'll be no peace until Gardner or Huff is in jail or dead.'

'Somebody should kill them.'

He glanced at her sidewise but she did not meet his eyes. She was looking at the back door of Doc Crow's office. He caught a glimpse of her profile, and it was set and determined, carrying a certain quality he had not met before in her makeup. He searched for a word to describe it and finally settled on stubbornness.

'Maybe somebody will.'

She had hold of his arm again, only this time her fingers did not dig. They seemed too possessive though.

'Buck, what are you going to do?'

He told her about the sheriff sending over his under-sheriff, one James McClellan. The farmers would wait until the law arrived. Then, if the lawman did nothing, they would take the matter into their own hands.

'But that might mean rifles and pistols and death, Buck.'

Buck nodded.

'What if Mrs. Lacey dies?'

She had voiced a fear that had been bothering the land locator ever since he had been notified about Frances Lacey being wounded.

'Then,' Buck said, 'we arm and move against the Rafter Y.'

'I hope she lives.'

'So do I,' said Buck. 'I pray she lives. Now you'd best get home, Laura. This wind is not too warm and you've been dancing all evening.'

'All right; for you, Buck.'

'Good girl.'

Buck went into the back room of Doc Crow's office. Jack Lacey had washed and he was pouring water down the sink. The water,

Buck noticed, was as red as though dye had been put in it.

Jack Lacey showed a swollen, beaten face. A black mouse was forming quickly under his left eye.

Buck said, 'Sure lots of black eyes on this range, Jack.'

Lacey turned and studied himself in the mirror. 'I have looked worse, Buck. One time a horse kicked me in the mug.'

'Wondered what had given you such a sour face,' Buck joked.

They sat on the bench. The door to the next room was shut, but they could hear Doc and Martha moving around. Now and then they heard Doc's guttural voice and Martha's answer.

Lacey said, 'All I can do is hope, Buck.'

Buck nodded.

They sat there, both silent. Buck found himself wondering if the farmer had accomplished anything substantial by whipping Cotter. Cotter would head for the Rafter Y and report this to Darr Gardner and Len Huff.

The land locator knew this all depended on whether or not Frances Lacey lived. On this range it was a hard offense to shoot a woman. And if she did live, the trouble would still be between his farmers and the cowmen. How

184

would it end?

Buck thought: It'll end with guns. It has to end that way. It's gone too far. Even if Under-Sheriff McClellan is honest and makes arrests on Gardner and Huff, it still has to end in guns, for they'll be back on this range in a few days. We have no concrete evidence against them.

Doc Crow came into the room, went to the wash basin and washed his hands. Jack Lacey waited for a second or two, giving the medico the first chance to speak, but Doc Crow just washed his hands.

'How is she, Doc?'

Doc did not look at the farmer. 'She'll be out of it in a few days. The wound was shallow and nothing vital was penetrated.'

'Thank heaven.'

Buck said, 'That's good. That sure is good news.'

CHAPTER SIXTEEN

When the barn had burned enough so the Rafter Y men could get close to it without danger, Darr Gardner had Len Huff organize a bucket brigade. Cowpunchers lined up between the windmill trough and the burning

185

buildings and buckets of water went along the line eventually to become dumped on the hot ashes.

It was gruelling, slow work. A bucket went down into the trough, then went along the line, slopping over as it moved from hand to hand. Then finally it reached the end of the line and ashes sizzled as the water hit them. And the dull smell of drenched coals arose, musty and strong.

Huff said, 'We could get shovels and cover them coals with dirt an' do it faster, Gardner.'

'Jus' keep the buckets movin'.'

Huff shrugged and went back to the windmill. The wind turned the fan and the water was lifted out of the earth, coming in spurts with each rise of the cylinder down deep in the well.

'What about it, Len?'

'He says to wet them ashes down, Shorty.'

'Needless work.'

'Tell him that, not me.'

Shorty looked at Darr Gardner, who was watching the coals. 'A hard man,' the cowpuncher murmured. 'Difficult to understand, he is.'

'He don't know his own mind,' growled Huff.

'I differ with you on that point.'

'Differ an' be blasted! Here, take this
186

bucket!'

The dawn moved across the land, a tawny tiger that took silent steps. The windmill squeaked, then slowed down. Finally it stopped completely. They dipped the tank down as far as they could, and then Huff said, 'That's all.'

Gardner came up. 'Tank dry?'

Huff wiped his hands on his overalls. 'She's dry, Gardner. And the wind has gone down. Now what?'

'Shovels.'

Huff said, 'The men have worked all night. That fire won't spread now. Most of them ashes has been soaked down. An' with the wind gone...'

'Get shovels from the blacksmith shop and get to work.'

Huff won a point. The shovels had all been in the old barn. They had moved them out of the blacksmith shop so there would be more space when a man went to do some smithy work. Now the shovels had been burned.

'You can see the steel bottom of one out there, Darr. See it stickin' up through them ashes?'

Gardner didn't look. 'Get your men on horseback and have them tromp them ashes flat. Some of 'em might be alive, even if they all got purty well wetted down. Tromp them into the soil.'

Huff asked, 'How about breakfast first?'

'Work 'em down. Now.'

Huff shrugged, but his eyes were too narrow. He went to where the Rafter Y riders stood and told them his boss's orders. There was some grumbling, but they went to the corral and got horses and saddled them.

Gardner walked to the house.

From there he watched his men riding the ashes into the earth. They looked like a bunch of Sioux bucks doing a war dance on horseback, their cayuses moving in and out. At last the site of the burned-down buildings was chopped up with horse hoofs and all the ashes had been ground into the earth and were dead.

The cook asked, 'Breakfast?'

Gardner nodded, not turning around. Many thoughts pounded across his brain, running in organized manner. This night had been a night of stirring events. And each event had crowded him and the farmers closer to open warfare.

He realized that these steps had been taken to scare the farmers. Now he would sit back for a spell and watch the effects of this night on the sodmen. Some, he felt sure, would leave, for these fires would put fear in them.

That would be good. When they left—if

they did leave—the odds would be lower against the Rafter Y. And when this was over he wanted to be alive. Not that he would sacrifice honor before a gunfight. A man had to live on a range, and if he ever turned the white feather he was through on that range.

Huff came in, stomping his feet on the mat on the porch, and he looked in with, 'That suit you?' His tone was sour.

Gardner said, 'Good work. That fire is out.'

'Should never have started.' Huff was gruff and displeased. He had spent a night in the saddle and once bullets had sung over him.

Gardner said, 'That's right, Len; but it was started.'

Huff stared at him, a thin man that was openly belligerent at this moment against his surroundings. Gardner read that the gunman was getting tense and his nerves were taut. Huff always got that way before he went into gunplay.

'Now who started it?'

Gardner said, 'Buck Wilson was one. Wilson is smart. Maybe he was alone; maybe he had help.'

'We shot at two riders,' Huff reminded him.

'Was one of them Wilson?'

Huff hung up his hat and rubbed his hands. 'I don't know. Looked like him in the

189

moonlight. But we was travelin' fast an' them two weren't standin' still, either. How about some chuck?'

'Here it comes.'

Usually Len Huff ate in the mess hall with the rest of the crew. Sometimes Gardner ate there, too, but those occasions were far apart. Huff snagged a chair and sat down at the table.

Gardner said, 'A drink?'

Huff nodded. 'Warm me up.' He cleared his throat.

Gardner got a bottle from the buffet and poured two whiskey glasses to the brim. Huff lifted his, looked at the amber liquid, and said, 'To us and to Burnt Wagon Basin. Years ago the Injuns hit a wagon train in this basin an' burned the wagons to the ground. Last night we burned a little ourself, an' got burned, too. Maybe we should change the name to Burnt Barn Basin.'

Gardner smiled over his glass. 'We'll take it up with the mayor of Burnt Wagon, an' call a special election.'

'The mayor,' intoned Huff, 'is too drunk to listen to us.'

Burnt Wagon had no mayor. Once the Rafter Y cowboys had proclaimed the swamper in the Cinch Ring Saloon the mayor of Burnt Wagon town. The swamper had been drunk and had been unconscious at the time, sleeping with his spittoons in the back room. He never was officially ordained the mayor. He never had a chance. He had died in his sleep, dead drunk.

Gardner drank, the whiskey warm in him. Then he sat down to a meal that consisted of eggs, bacon, and hotcakes, with plenty of coffee. The combination of food and whiskey made a glow in him.

'Len, we got them on the run.'

'I think so, Gardner. Especially if we winged one of them gents we tangled with this mornin'. We kill a farmer or two an' the rest will grow chicken feathers an' fly screechin' an' cacklin' outa the basin.'

'Hope you're right.'

'I know I'm right.'

'You've made a few errors.'

'Dang few though.' Huff balanced a forkful of hotcake. 'Biggest error I made was down in Texas when I should have married that squaw an' let that white battle axe ride past me.'

'Wonder where Caroline is?'

Huff chewed his hotcake. 'Wherever she is, she is making some man's life miserable. Sometimes it seemed as if that woman just loved to make me feel bad. Well, she's a thing of the past, too.'

They ate.

Somewhere, hoofs sounded.

Huff said, looking out the window, 'Man jes' rid in, Gardner. From here he looks like Cotter. You had him in town for a spy, didn't you?'

'Yes.'

Huff said casually, 'Cotter never told you about them farmers meetin' last night. Cotter had no way to find that out.'

'You still worried about that?'

'Not worried, but curious.'

'Stay that-a-way, then.'

From where Gardner sat he could not see Cotter. Huff angled his head around so he could see better.

'Cotter's sure rid that bronc hard.'

'He's found out something down in town. He comin' up to the house?'

'Yeah, he's comin' this . . . Man, look at his face! He looks like a herd of buffaler has stampeded over him!'

Gardner did not get out of his chair, although curiosity was strong in him. Only when Cotter stood in the doorway did the owner of the Rafter Y look up, and then it seemed with only a casual interest.

'Did you win?'

Cotter said, 'Yeah, I won. I won second.'

'Who won first?'

'Jack Lacey.'

192

'What did you two fight about?'

'Somebody shot Lacey's woman. From what I could gather them two had rid down to their barn when it was on fire. Then they circled wide lookin' for sign. They run into two riders, an' guns talked, and the woman stopped a slug.'

Huff said, 'My Gawd, this is it!'

Gardner's face was impassive. But behind that hard mask ran the smooth tug and pull of his thoughts. Cotter did not know that he and Len Huff had exchanged shots with the Laceys. Cotter only knew that two riders had come out of the night, met the Laceys, and short-guns and rifles had talked.

And a woman had been shot . . .

Gardner thought: This is the straw that breaks the camel's back.

'Tell it from the start, Cotter.'

Cotter did.

Len Huff walked to the window and stared into the dawn of the new day. He could not keep himself in one spot. Unrest demanded he break his line of thoughts by the familiar action of physical movement.

Huff looked out the window, his face moody as he listened. Then, those thoughts pestering him, he turned and walked to the other window.

'Sit down, Len,' ordered Gardner. 'Be

quiet.'

Huff studied him. 'You try to boss my movements even? Is that it?'

'You're nervous; sit down.'

'This is it,' Huff said.

Cotter looked at him. Darr Gardner looked at him.

'A woman has been shot,' Huff went on. 'You can fight a man on this range but men can't fight a woman. Don't ask me why, but that's the way it is.'

Gardner nodded. 'Go on, Len.'

'Well, Missus Lacey got shot. That puts all the farmers against us in earnest. That unites them all. None of them can leave now. No man can run off and leave a woman who's been shot.'

Cotter said, 'That's right, Huff.'

'Had a man been shot, they'd have acted different. But a man didn't get plugged. A woman got shot.'

Gardner said, 'Sit down, Len.'

Huff smiled, and said, 'I've had my talk.'

Huff sat down. He added this up, and the sum was always the same. But in a way, maybe it had been for the best. Now this problem would be solved and guns would solve it and the solution would be brought about soon.

Cotter said, 'I'll get some chuck in the mess

194

hall and tell the boys, Gardner.'

Gardner nodded.

Cotter left, spurs making their noises. From the chair Len Huff watched the cowpuncher bowleg his way to the mess shack. When Cotter was out of sight in the building, Huff looked at Darr Gardner.

'Well, Gardner?'

'This is it,' Gardner said.

'We ride in with our men.'

Gardner nodded.

Huff said, 'Cotter didn't mention hearin' anybody say that it was you an' me who traded shots with the Laceys.'

'Maybe they didn't recognize us, Len.'

Huff gave this a quick going-over in his mind. Then he sighed and said, 'Well, what diff does it make?' He answered his own question. 'Every farmer knows it was two Rafter Y men who shot at the Laceys, even though they might not know for sure them two men was us.'

Gardner nodded.

Huff repeated, 'This is it, sure as shootin'.'

Gardner got to his feet. He had been in the saddle all night, but Cotter's words seemed to have ripped all idea of sleep out of his mind. Without a word, he went out of the house, and Huff watched him go to the corral. Gardner got down his rope and laid it across the neck of

195

a sorrel and saddled him and rode alone toward town.

Huff watched him leave, and Huff had a frown of wonder. Now where was Gardner going and why did he ride alone? Huff thought: Maybe I should go with him, and then he remembered that Darr Gardner had not asked him to accompany him.

So Huff remained at the Rafter Y.

Gardner rode out in a circle, following the rim of the hills. This way he could watch the terrain below him and yet could not be seen by a rider who watched the hills. He saw Dick Smith leave his farm on Cottonwood Creek and turn his buggy toward the homestead of Tim McCarty, across the ridge on Summit Creek. He watched the fat man through his field glasses.

Yonder, miles away a rider moved, going from one homestead shack to the other, and Gardner knew that the man was spreading word among the farmers about the shooting of Frances Lacey. The rider had already been to Dick Smith's house, and Smith had gone over to talk to McCarty, Darr figured.

The Rafter Y man held his bronc to a halt in the protection of a giant sandstone rock and his face went soft as he looked down on Burnt Wagon Basin. The valley unfolded below him, green and marked by the gentle hand of spring and spring rains, running farther and farther from his sight, until its edges became part of the hills, until the hills rose in majesty to become the Little Rockies.

Once that basin had been his, and his cattle had grazed where they had pleased. Now the smoothness of it was broken by fence posts and barbed wire, by the darkness where the plow had turned the soil, burying the native buffalo grass. Now the basin was not his, and he and his holdings were fighting for their existence.

He did not realize that he was, in reality, not fighting the farmers, but that his opponent was progress, and the farmers were just representatives of this westward progress. A nation was moving westward toward its destiny, and the outer boundaries of that destiny were to the West, always West. Steel had spanned a nation, and locomotives moved across that steel, smoke spewing forth from their odd-shaped smoke-stacks, and these rails had cut down the time it required to move from coast to coast.

Gardner did not recognize these facts, because he did not know them. He had been knocked from pillar to post as a child, and this had marked his manhood—a giant finger had come down and marked his personality with one word, *greed*. Now this destroying trait of

197

his character—this trait sired by an unfortunate childhood and adolescence—was written across his face as he gazed silently down at Burnt Wagon Basin.

A voice behind said, 'Darr.'

Gardner turned, seemingly not surprised. 'What do you know?'

'You're to the point, sir.'

Gardner said, 'Well?'

The rider said, 'Mrs. Lacey got shot.'

'I know that. Cotter told me that. But there's more than that.'

'Cotter took a terrible beating from Lacey.'

Gardner was not looking at the rider now. 'I rode along the hills so you could see me. I held up operations until I could talk to you. Now all you tell me is something I already know.'

'Your will?'

Darr Gardner said, 'They won't kill this man.'

'You don't know. I'm playing this close. You haven't changed that will?'

'Who would I name in place of you?'

'All right, Gardner, all right. Here's what I know. Under-Sheriff James McClellan is riding into Burnt Wagon. He should be in town within a few days. Wilson told me that.'

'That makes no difference. McClellan will look around, make a report to the sheriff that everything is normal. McClellan knows who buys the butter for his bread, and that butter is awful thick right now.'

'Well, that's number one.'

'Number two?'

'Buck Wilson's farmers are ready to fight. When the Rafter Y shot that woman, that bullet sure organized the farmers. Wilson sent a man out to tell them. They hold a meeting in town this afternoon.'

'We could burn.'

'What good would it do you? Burn or no burn, they'll move against you. I'm sure of that. So is Buck Wilson.'

'They'll move,' Gardner conceded.

There was a silence. Both of them looked down into Burnt Wagon Basin. The wind moved through the rocks, giving out an eerie song. It rubbed against Gardner's nerves suddenly. He wanted to get away from this spot. He wanted to leave this rider. He remembered Len Huff, walking the floor, moving from window to window. Huff was on edge. Huff was ready.

He himself was now in the same mood. He knew now, for sure, that this day would see the end of this trouble. He looked across the basin, he looked at the mountains, and he glanced at the sun. The earth was good and the mountains were good and the sun was strong.

The rider said, 'That's all.'

'Thanks.'

The rider turned horse and said, 'Good luck, and lots of it.'

'We'll need it.'

Nothing more was said. The rider moved back into the hills. A few minutes later, Gardner looked around. He looked at the hills and he ran his eyes along ravines. Still he could not see the rider.

The disappearance of the rider had been brought about so quickly and so completely that Darr Gardner expelled a breath of admiration. That rider could come out of nowhere to kill a man and then as swiftly return to nowhere. Greed motivated that rider and greed motivated him and this bound them with an unbreakable bond.

But the Rafter Y owner did not dwell long on these thoughts. At the present they held small space when he matched them against the ever-present threat of the Wilson farmers.

When this farmer trouble had been settled, then there would be time to handle this rider. Until this solution was accomplished the main problem was the Burnt Wagon hoemen.

Gardner noticed that farmers were moving toward Burnt Wagon town, rigs and men on horseback being drawn into the town by the strong magnet of trouble.

200

They were leaving their buildings unguarded. This trouble had got to a point where property did not count. What was at stake was the right of a man to breathe, to work and live peacefully. And to establish this right these farmers were ready to fight.

Gardner showed a grin, and rode down the slope. He had found out the information he had sought. The showdown was at hand.

He came into the Rafter Y in mid-forenoon. His men had been kept at the home ranch by Len Huff. This was no day to ride bog holes, to turn cattle back from the far limits of the Rafter Y.

Huff came forward. 'Well, boss?'

Gardner jerked the latigo free and unsaddled his sorrel. 'This is it,' he said shortly. 'Wilson has summoned them into town. They're going to make up their mind to hit us. But we beat them to it.'

'How?'

'We're in town when they hold the meetin'!'

Huff nodded, his eyes dull. 'Some of the boys won't ride with us.'

'How many?'

'About five.'

Gardner measured his men who stood in front of the bunk house. He went over to them, walking slowly, his hand on his gun.

'Who won't ride with us?'

They were silent for a long time. Darr Gardner's eyes moved from man to man, judging them, watching them.

'Who won't ride?'

A slim man said, 'I won't.'

Gardner studied him. 'Why not, Jackson?'

'My life means somethin' to me. I don't want to die for a cow.'

Another said, 'I think the same, Gardner.'

Gardner didn't take his eyes off Jackson. 'You're not workin' for a cow. You're workin' for me. You draw my wages an' I'm your boss.'

'I hired to punch cows. This grass'll be here after we're both gone. I don't aim to die for it, Gardner.'

They eyed each other. Gardner had his hand on his holstered gun, and Jackson had his hand on his Colt, too.

Gardner said, 'You a coward?'

'No.'

Gardner said suddenly, 'All right, you men who don't want to ride into town, get your private broncs and ride out. Don't be on this range when we come back from town, savvy?'

Five men walked into the bunkhouse, Jackson leading them. The others went for their broncs and saddles. They mounted and Gardner looked them over, then said to Huff,

202

'We've got enough.'
'Let's ride an' quit gabbin'!'

CHAPTER SEVENTEEN

They took Frances Lacey to the hotel, carrying the wounded woman on Doc Crow's stretcher. Buck was at one end of the stretcher and Doc was at the other. Dawn was clear and the morning was on them.

Jack Lacey walked beside the stretcher. The farmer's wife was still under the spell of ether and she lay on her back, breathing steadily, her eyes closed. Townspeople stood along the plank sidewalks and watched, their curiosity making them dumb.

They came into the hotel and the old proprietor came around the counter, acting as though he would not let them enter with an unconscious woman. But Jack Lacey looked at him and asked, 'Well, fella?'

'Come on in.'

Jack Lacey looked back at Buck and grinned. Buck winked.

Doc Crow said, 'Let's get her into bed. This end of this thing is heavy. All I've done the last few days is carry around unconscious people.'

'Want the room next to Hatfield?' the

proprietor asked.

'That's good,' Buck replied.

They went down the hall and the old man opened the door to the room adjoining that of the fur buyer. Doc had Jack Lacey hold his end of the stretcher and the medico got the woman on the bed.

'You men are done.'

Lacey moved over. He bent down and kissed his wife on the mouth. The gesture was simple and spoke of a great love. Buck and Lacey left silently, and the land locator was glad for silence.

Buck said, 'I'm going in to see Hatfield.'

'I'll go with you.'

Hatfield was sitting in a chair eating his breakfast. He was glad to see them, and his wide face showed a good-natured smile.

'When you gettin' on your feet, Glen?' Jack Lacey wanted to know.

'Doc says a few more days until I get around. But dang it, men, I'm getting tired of this room. I want to get out and stake out that homestead of mine, what with spring here.'

The fur buyer spoke to Buck now. 'I wrote my wife about me going to take up a homestead. I got a hunch she'll be right happy, Wilson.'

Lacey looked at Buck. 'Tell him, Buck?'

Buck said, 'He'd find out sooner or later,

204

and he might just as well know the truth.' He then told the fur buyer about two night riders shooting Frances Lacey. Hatfield listened in surprise, mouth open a little. His own troubles and pain seemed submerged under this greater shock. Buck also told him about Rafter Y men burning down Horace Browning's barn.

'Some property at the Rafter Y got burnt too,' Jack Lacey said.

'Who burned that?' Hatfield asked.

They both looked at Buck, who grinned. 'I don't know,' he said.

They all laughed softly, reading the implication in his remark. Then Hatfield's face became heavy as he looked at Jack Lacey. Buck knew that the fur buyer and Lacey were good friends, although they had not known each other very long. Hatfield had used the Lacey farm as an office while he had been out buying furs and hides off the other farmers.

'What are you going to do, Jack?'

Buck also looked at Lacey. Hatfield had, by his direct question, put Lacey in a position where he would have to tell what he intended to do; whether he would strike back personally at the Rafter Y, or wait until the law arrived in Burnt Wagon.

But Jack Lacey evaded it with, 'I'll make up my mind, mebbe . . .'

Glen Hatfield looked at Buck.

Hatfield said, 'Frances is a mighty fine woman, Jack.'

'Thanks, Glen.'

Hatfield's eyes showed defeat. 'Don't do anything rash, Jack, until the farmers arrive and you talk this over in a body.'

Lacey did not answer.

They went outside, and the sunlight was strong and clean. The earth was drying, sending up its aromas and its promises. The bell rang in the school house, summoning the people to church, for the traveling minister held church each Sunday.

Lacey said, 'I have to do somethin', Buck, or go crazy. I'm going to ride from farm to farm to get the farmers into town. What time shall I set a meetin' for?'

'As soon as they all get here,' Buck said.

Lacey went toward the livery barn. Buck was restless himself, and yet in the core of him there was a great sorrow, an unvoiced fear. He knew that hoemen, when they had learned that the Rafter Y had shot a woman, would come into town armed and ready for warfare.

Maybe some of them would not see the sun tomorrow at this hour.

That thought hurt him. He wondered if he could call Gardner and have it out with the Rafter Y boss without getting the farmers into this fight. He did not want any of his hoemen killed.

He played with that thought, rolling it over in his mind. He tasted of it and it was bitter. Still, it was a thought, and out of it might come a plan. He put it against the wall of his mind and let it rest.

He saw Martha Buckman cross the street, going toward church. He remembered the look that had been in Jack Lacey's eyes, and he wondered if that look were in his eyes now that he saw Martha. His decision had been made—this unrest had left him.

'Will you go to church with me, Buck?'

'With this trouble over me, Martha? Would it be right?'

Her blue eyes were on him. 'That is why man has a church and a religion, Buck. Churches are meant to help those in trouble.'

Buck said, 'Martha, I love you.'

'I'm glad of that, Buck.'

Her arm was in his.

'I'm not dressed up for church.'

'Come along, Buck, just as you are. Minister Swanson will be glad to see you in his gathering.'

Afterwards Buck and Martha talked to the young minister for a few minutes. The congregation had left and the three of them were alone in the schoolhouse. The young minister knew of the trouble this basin was having.

Buck told him about last night. He told about the sheriff sending over an under-sheriff.

The minister was frank. 'I doubt if that under-sheriff will do much. The whole thing is a gesture to clear the county seat of further blame.'

Buck said, 'Then what do we do, reverend?'

'Do what your conscience and your character demand, Buck.'

'But that would mean war.'

The young man gathered up his papers and his Bible. 'I am a man who committed himself to help humanity through God's word. There are some problems that cannot be settled except through strife, sir.'

Buck said, 'Thank you, sir.'

'God be with you, Mr. Wilson. I am glad I have been of help, as small as my help has been. And good day to you, Miss Buckman.'

Buck felt better when he left, Martha's hand in his. Sunshine washed across this land, promising a better tomorrow, and somewhere a meadow lark sang, its throat golden and breaking with praise.

'Have you had breakfast?'

Buck said, 'Gosh, I forgot all about eating. And I'm hungry, too. But let's not go to your place. We'll wake up your mother.'

'She's awake by now.'

Buck shook his head. 'We'll eat at the Broken Spur, Martha. Your mother would ask me too many questions.'

'All right with me.'

Wong Ling hovered over them, keeping up a chatter. They had always been what he called 'his kids,' and now that danger was in the air he was much more protective.

'You give me an' Hatchet Joe some guns, an' by golly this thing will be finished very fast an' very pronto.'

'Sure can see where you stand,' Buck said. 'Now can that chatter an' bring us some chuck.'

'Free meal on me,' the Chinese said, paddling back to his kitchen. 'No Lafter Y men in town, or me cuttem their thloats, by golly.' He mumbled something in a sing-song Chinese that neither of them understood.

'There's Hatchet Joe now,' Martha said.

Buck's handyman was dismounting from his mule in front of the store. He had a big .45 strapped around his skinny waist and he carried an old Civil War rifle, a heavy affair.

Buck said, 'He's ready for anythin', he is.'

Hatchet Joe saw them through the window of the Broken Spur and came in, gear clanging.

'Lacey, he see me. Tell me about troubles, Buck. I ride fast as grasshopper into town. Other farmers they come, too. Later. 'I go visit Wong Ling.'

Hatchet Joe clattered back into the kitchen. Buck and Martha heard the two Chinese sawing back and forth in their native tongue. Once Hatchet Joe had told Buck that he had difficulty in understanding Wong Ling's Chinese. Evidently excitement made the other understandable, for they talked like a house afire. Or, as Buck Wilson reflected, a *barn* on fire.

Martha and Buck finished eating, neither saying much. Both understood the other on one particular point, and this amounted to a lot to Buck right now. He knew that Martha was worried about him, but he knew she would say nothing to try to change his opinion.

He didn't feel too happy, himself. He had just discovered a great thing, something that *might* change his life forever—he used the word *might* with reservations for a bullet didn't care what it hit—a wall or the dust or a man's flesh. Then he realized maybe he was trying to think too far ahead.

There might be a chance that Gardner and Huff, realizing the farmers were united against them, might pull back their horns.

There was this chance, although Buck figured it was an outside chance, meager at best.

But you never knew what the other fellow would do.

Martha said, 'I hope the Rafter Y draws back, Buck.'

'So do I.' The land locator grinned boyishly.

Wong Ling and Hatchet Joe were so busy sing-songing that they did not hear the couple go. Buck walked to the end of the street with her. There, behind a building, he said, 'Wait a minute.'

'Yes?'

She was in his arms, then. She was soft and yielding and womanly. Her lips were warm and moist and good. Finally she stepped back.

'Be careful, Buck.'

'I sure will.'

She had tears in her eyes. Before she really started to weep, though, she had turned and was gone, running toward home. Buck went back on the main street, and he didn't feel any too good.

He went to his office.

Sitting in his chair, he gave this matter deep thought. This whole town was tense on this Sunday morning. Residents were sitting back and watching, expectant, nervous. The entire country was in the grip of fear. They were not

211

afraid of him or his farmers. They were not afraid of the Rafter Y.

They were afraid of the aftermath—the death and destruction—that this trouble would bring.

He had little respect for these townsmen and women. With the exception of Martha and a few others, they had all been against his bringing in farmers and, now that the farmers were here, they were still against them. Openly they showed their antagonism and dislike for the sodmen.

All he wanted them to do was to stand back and stay neutral. But if one of them picked up a rifle to aid the Rafter Y . . . Those would be big odds—the Rafter Y and the townsmen combined—but Buck knew he and his sodmen would fight them. Furthermore, now that Frances Lacey had been shot, the land locator figured the town would stay neutral.

In fact, he wondered if the fact that the Rafter Y had shot a woman had not switched some of the local feeling toward the side of him and his farmers. It was one thing to shoot a man, another thing to shoot a woman.

A buggy stopped in the alley, and he heard Dick Smith's voice. He did not go to the window. A few minutes later Dick Smith waddled in, rifle in hand. Behind him came Tim McCarty, beefy and red of face.

McCarty also carried a Winchester. Around his girth was a gunbelt and his .45 was tied down with a rawhide thong that encircled his thick thigh.

'Jack Lacey was out to tell us,' Smith said.

'Sit down,' Buck said.

Dick Smith said, 'I need some .45 shells.'

'We'll get some, if we need some,' Buck said.

Smith and McCarty sat on the bench. The stamp of this was on their faces, almost a brand. They were heavy and glum, but yet under that laziness was something quick and fine and clean and alert. Buck felt this and found strength in it.

'How's Mrs. Lacey?' asked Dick Smith.

Buck told them the extent of the woman's wounds. He told them all he knew about the case and they listened in silence, although he knew he was only repeating what they had heard from Jack Lacey.

'Too bad,' Tim McCarty said. ''Tis a nice woman she is, too.'

'Gardner's doin' his own spyin',' Smith said.

Buck looked inquiringly at the heavy rancher.

'When we went over to Tim's, I saw a rider way off in the distance. My field glasses showed him to me like he was Darrell Gardner himself. But I'm not sure, for 'twas a long distance.'

'He's got spies,' Buck said.

Tim McCarty said, 'Now what if they sneak in while we are gone and fire our barns and belongings, Buck? All of the farms will be deserted, for I suppose Mrs. Sherman will come to town with her Spike.'

'We'll head for the Rafter Y,' Buck said.

Tim sent him a coy, sidewise glance. 'And now who was it, Buckley, that fired the Rafter Y barns last night, might I ask?'

'You got me,' Buck said, smiling.

Dick Smith said, 'Now it couldn't have been Buck Wilson and one Horace Browning? No, it couldn't have been them, could it?'

'Perish the thought,' Buck said.

They sat there with only small talk passing between them. Time dragged by, moving on slow feet; the clock ticked, and outside, the wind moved against the corner of the building.

Spike Sherman came in and said, 'Howdy, men.'

'Howdy, boy.'

''Lo, Spike.'

'Sit down,' Buck said.

The young farmer sat down beside Dick Smith but he spoke to them all. 'Shannon wouldn't stay at the farm alone with the baby, so I took them into town. We were down to see Mrs. Lacey, but she's purty sick. Doc says that ether hit her hard. Shannon and the baby went over to Martha's, Buck.'

Buck nodded.

Spike Sherman glanced at the others, seeing their arms. He wore a gunbelt and pistol, and he had put his rifle against the wall when he had entered. He put out his legs and seemed to be interested in his boots.

'Lacey sure trimmed that Cotter fella, huh, Buck?'

'He did all right.'

'Jake should be in soon,' Sherman said. Nobody answered and he rolled a cigarette and lit it, but the taste of it must have been bad, for he took only a few drags before he ground the head off against the bench.

Jake Jones was the next man, moving his small bulk through the door. He said hello and put his rifle beside that of Sherman and took his seat, asking the usual questions about Frances Lacey. These answered, he was very quiet, and his thin face reflected the seriousness of his thoughts.

Ten minutes later, Horace Browning and Jack Lacey entered together. Browning nodded, silent and sincere, and Jack Lacey said, 'The Rafter Y is comin' toward town. We seen the riders from the ridge just as we come into town.'

Buck asked, 'How many riders?'

'How many, Horace?'

'We counted ten, an' that includes Gardner an' Huff.'

Buck said, 'They have the odds in manpower. All right, here it is, men. They're ridin' to town because they know we are meetin' here.'

'How would they know?' Spike Sherman demanded. 'Is there a spy in this bunch?'

'They knew about the meetin' last night at your place,' Dick Smith rumbled. His heavy eyes touched each man present.

Buck said, 'I'm sure there's no spy here. Somebody has been spyin' on us, but that ain't the problem now. They're better gunmen than we are. The law is on our side. We take to the roofs and when they ride in we surprise them, savvy?'

'Good idea, Buck.'

'Let's go, men.'

Buck said, 'Get behind the false fronts and scatter out. That way we'll have them penned.'

'And you?' a man asked.

Buck said, grinning, 'Don't worry about me, Tim.'

CHAPTER EIGHTEEN

Darr Gardner looked at his riders and let a silence grow. Then he said, 'Well, here we are, on the outskirts of Burnt Wagon. We've talked this over and each man knows his job is to kill as many farmers as he can.'

They were grim and tough and ready. They were saddlemen at a showdown, and they had their Colts loaded, their Winchesters full of cartridges. They looked at him and they were silent.

Gardner said, 'I'll go over this again,' and he hooked his left leg around his saddle-horn and lit his cigarette. His horse stood rock still. Gardner talked in a low voice, his cigarette bobbing as it hung to his underlip.

'We split up. Len Huff takes one-half of you men and goes down the west side of the main street. I take the other half and cover the east side of the strip. This way we converge onto Buck Wilson's office.

'Kill each and every farmer you can see. Remember to shoot to kill, for they'll shoot to kill you. There's no use stuffin' ourselves. Them farmers know we're ridin' into town. They're no fools. Their guards have told them we're ridin' in.

'They might be scattered, and they might not be. We got to play this game close, therefore we move in on foot like an army takin' over a town. Take your time and use your weapons.

'We have two bywords. When in doubt of a man's identity, holler the word *Milk River*. If a man answers with the words *Burnt Wagon*, then he's one of us, savvy?'

Huff said, 'Let's get goin'!'

They went down and Winchesters slid out of saddle boots. Bootheels punched holes in the damp, clean earth. Rifle breeches slid open, cartridges slid into barrels, and then the breeches closed. Thumbs pushed levers on the safety click.

Gardner looked at Huff and said, 'You know your job. Get Wilson as soon as you can. I'll try for the same. We get him and the head is chopped off the snake. Without a head, a snake ain't got no fangs.'

'I know my part!'

Huff snarled the words. He was raw and tense, and he knew that when the gunsmoke floated, only then would he be loose and deadly. That was the way he acted against danger. When he went toward danger his muscles were knotted and bunched, tight and with little movement. Then the guns talked and they limbered and his brain became clear

218

as a placid mountain lake.

Gardner said, 'Good luck to all of you.'

'Same to you, boss.'

They moved off then, leaving their broncs ground-tied in the brush, and behind Gardner came his men. They had kicked off spurs and chaps so they would make less noise as they moved between buildings and down the alleys.

They said nothing.

They took the alley on the east side of Burnt Wagon's main street. Gardner looked to the west. He could not see Len Huff and Huff's men. Already they had entered the shacks and buildings that made up that side of the town's limits.

They came into the alley and Gardner said, 'Spread out, and fight, you scissorbills! Spread out!'

They drifted into old sheds and outbuildings, and began working their way toward Buck Wilson's office. The town was quiet and some of the women and children and even a few of the men had left. Gardner had seen them walking out of town and knew they would watch from a nearby hill.

Gardner did not know that Buck Wilson had put his farmers on top of roofs along the main street. Had he known this, he would have put his men onto buildings, and the battle would have been fought there.

He heard a rifle spit, and another rifle answered. That was across the main stem, and he knew Huff had met the enemy. Then, from behind him, a short-gun roared, and he heard one of his own men scream, 'They're on the roofs! One of 'em jus' shot me!'

A rifle talked, a short-gun answered, and the man did not holler again. Quick as a panther, Darr Gardner pulled in flat against a building.

'Milk River,' Gardner hollered.

A man called, 'Burnt Wagon.'

Gardner said, 'Where are they?'

'On the roofs,' the voice answered.

The cry went from man to man: 'On the roofs! On the roofs along the main street! Milk River! Burnt Wagon!'

Gardner ordered, 'Climb, Rafter Y men, climb!'

Gardner himself did not climb. He pulled close to the building and waited and listened and made his plans. The logs were rough against him, he pushed that close to them.

Sporadic gunfire sounded, coming in sudden bursts as men matched rifles. From the corner of the Cinch Ring Saloon a Rafter Y man came down, falling hard and landing hard.

He did not move.

He was about fifty feet away from Gardner.

Looking at him, Gardner thought, 'Well, Johnnie's dead.' That was as far as the thought went. Sympathy did not color it.

The wind moved in and stirred Johnnie's shirt slightly. Then the wind moved on, impartial and thoughtless.

Gardner knew he would have to move down that alley and get to Buck Wilson's office. That building was a magnet at the end of the alley, pulling him toward it. He figured Wilson would be somewhere around the building.

Why?

He didn't know. He just figured that way.

He moved ahead, going slowly, rifle ready. He went to another building, stopped there, listened. Rifles were cracking more steadily now, and a bullet went wild down the alley. Gardner pulled back and waited, peering ahead.

Then he saw the man come off the shed. He came from Wilson's office, sliding down the roof to the shed. He was bent over and he moved quickly. But Gardner recognized Buck Wilson.

Gardner shot, rifle rising with one movement. But the man had moved too quickly. Gardner cursed to himself, 'I missed.'

Gardner was very calm. He gave this setup a quick and accurate scrutiny. Directly across the street was the highest building in town, the hotel. Across from it—the building that shielded him—was the hardware store.

He figured that a Rafter Y rifleman on the hardware store had flushed Buck Wilson out of cover on the land locator's office. In this surmise Darr Gardner was right. Len Huff was on the hardware store roof.

Huff had run Buck off the adjoining roof.

Now Gardner waited, figuring that Buck would come off the back of the roof, for if he went over the front, the land locator would have to cross the street under the threat of Huff's rifle. Therefore logic told him Wilson would run out into the alley.

But Buck fooled the Rafter Y boss.

He had shot Len Huff in the leg, making it hard for Huff to walk. But Huff, he knew, did not need two good legs to shoot a rifle, and Huff was therefore very dangerous yet.

The rifle bullet singing over him had told him a man was also in the alley. Therefore he went over the side of his building. He landed hard, still hanging onto his rifle, and he circled the front of his office, sprinting across that space.

A bullet came from down the street, and Buck heard glass break in his office. Then he was in the slot between the hardware store and the cafe. Huff was over him, and Huff had a rifle and a good shooting eye.

But this way, he'd come in behind the man in the alley.

He put his rifle against the wall, for this would be close work, and he wanted his pistol. The rifle would be hard to turn and unwieldy. He drew in a deep breath, then stepped into the alley, pistol in hand.

Nobody was on the strip ahead of him!

For Darr Gardner had run across the alley and gone between two buildings. This hid him and put him a little behind Buck. Gardner was not new to this warfare, and this maneuver showed his cunning.

Gardner said, 'Buck Wilson, turn!'

The rest was lost in the smash of the Rafter Y man's rifle. He did not give the land locator a chance to turn. Gardner's rifle was up to his shoulder and he stood wide-legged, taking in its sights.

The bullet hit Buck Wilson in the right ribs. A thousand horses seemed to kick him; his breath was knocked from him. It turned him and he faced Gardner. Then the land locator realized he was on his knees.

Buck was very sick, and Gardner shot again. He missed this time and Buck saw dust sprout, but he gave it no thought. His only

223

thought was to get his pistol working, to kill this man who had ambushed him.

He felt the gun kick, but it did not seem that the handle moved against his flesh, for it had no shock. He remembered shooting again, and he remembered seeing Darr Gardner drop the rifle.

Gardner's mouth was wide, and still no cries came. The rifle clattered, hitting some tin cans, and Gardner went back. He stood against the shed and he said, 'Wilson, you've killed me.'

Buck was on the ground, and he didn't know how he got there. Sickness washed in with a surging nausea, and the next thing he knew Gardner was down. That thought held strength, but yet it was a weak thought.

Dust rose beside him, and he rolled over with difficulty. He got to his feet, lurched to the shed, and a bullet hit him in the calf of his leg. He realized that Len Huff was shooting from the top of the hardware store.

He could not see Len Huff. The man, he realized, was behind the wall, for the wall extended up a few feet above the roof, with spouts out for rain water to run down.

Huff can kill me, he thought.

That thought, strangely, held no terror. He was wounded badly, he knew. He could not run, nor did he want to run. He wanted to get

Huff, for Huff had shot him. That was the main thought.

He saw the edge of a man's shirt and he shot at it, deliberately placing his bullet now. He saw splinters fly out of the railing. Huff shot again, and a bullet hit the wall beside him.

A man behind him hollered, 'I'm coverin' him from here, Huff. Between us we'll kill that son!'

He was a jackrabbit, wounded and bloody, caught between two wolves.

Huff said, 'We'll get him!'

Buck waited, and then, across the street, he saw a rifle kick out the pane of a window. It came steadily outward and settled across the sill. The rifleman was behind Huff and over him and he shot with a cold precision.

Huff stood up, tried to say something. Then he fell from the roof, twisting like a falling leaf. But a leaf hits the ground lightly . . .

Buck saw the thick face of Glen Hatfield behind the rifle. Then, for the second time, he was tasting dust.

Gunfire moved away into a remote, distant land, and then died in the ears of land locator Buck Wilson.

*   *   *

A week later, Buck Wilson and Martha Buckman were married, with Buck standing on crutches. Glen Hatfield was the best man and he had a big hand hooked under Buck's arm to steady him.

By that time, law and order had come to Burnt Wagon. The territorial governor had moved fast, ousted the Chinook sheriff, and had called a special election. They had tried to get Buck to take the office.

'Heck, boys,' he had said, 'I'm goin' to get married. I'm a farmer, not a lawman. How about Dick Smith?'

'Smith'd make a good sheriff.'

Buck and Martha were married in the schoolhouse with the Reverend Swanson performing the ceremony. Buck would limp until the day he died.

'Do you take this man...'

'I do.'

Buck thought of Horace Browning, who had been killed in the Burnt Wagon fight, and a hard lump was in his throat. But Jack Lacey, both arms in slings, grinned at him, and Frances Lacey, on her feet by now, gave Buck a big wink.

'Do you, Buckley Wilson, take this woman...'

'I do.'

The Rafter Y was no more. Darr Gardner

was dead, and so was Len Huff, and Laura Fromberg had sold the Rafter Y cattle to a Black Hills outfit, who were rounding up the brand's stock and moving them toward the Bad Lands of Dakota Territory.

For Laura Fromberg had been Darr Gardner's sister. Her real name had been Laura Gardner, but she had changed it for the time being, coming into Burnt Wagon presumably to teach school, but in reality to spy on the farmers.

Buck had unwittingly supplied her with information and she in return had relayed this to Darr Gardner.

Laura Fromberg had left Burnt Wagon right after her brother had been killed. From the county seat at Chinook she had hurriedly probated Gardner's will, taken possession, and then had sold the big ranch's cattle.

She never returned to Burnt Wagon.

The whole deal left the entire county astounded. But, as Tim McCarty said, 'A man cain't never tell about a woman.'

'Or a man either,' Mrs. Hatfield said hurriedly.

She had moved out to be with her husband. She was a fat woman, always smiling, and she had taken Martha and Buck into her big heart. Now she stood on Martha's right, acting as matron-of-honor.

227

'I now pronounce you man and wife.'

Reverend Swanson bowed his head and led them in prayer. He prayed for the dead men on each side, and Buck listened with a heavy heart. Then he and Martha were being helped into the double-seated spring wagon.

'All set, Buck?' asked Spike Sherman, grinning.

'Okay, Spike.'

'We're comin' behind you,' Frances Lacey said, 'and the wedding dance starts as soon as we get to your farm, Buck.'

Hatchet Joe turned in the front seat, holding the lines. 'All set, boss?'

'Let 'er rip, Joe!'

The Chinese lashed his team and the buggy lurched, shooting out into the road. Behind them people hollered and yipped and ran for their rigs to follow. Hatchet Joe drove at a lope.

Once he looked back.

Martha was in Buck's arms, and her lips were against his. Then the lurching buckboard jerked them apart and Buck saw Hatchet Joe's wide grin.

'Grin, go on. See if I care,' he teased.

Hatchet Joe turned around. He hollered back, 'Me velly happy!'

'Who isn't?' Buck wanted to know.

228